Huntress

Book One of the Deadlands Duology

Devin Thorpe

For those who've been made to feel weak by this world. May you find your inner hellcat and stand up for yourself.

CONTENTS

GLOSSARY

Areopagus – The central kingdom in this world; the Areopagus is home to the Sylvians' long-established reign over the many fiefdoms in its immediate control.

Blackblood Virus – A vicious pandemic that swept over the Undead civilization centuries ago; the Blackblood virus is an infectious disease that turns Undead into demon spawn. The virus turns the blood in their veins black, but it also perverts their minds and fills them with unquenchable bloodlust.

Cardone – An ancient city that exists no more; Cardone was once the central kingdom that ruled the nation until a war between Dagon and Damon broke out, reducing its buildings to rubble and its population to genocide.

Creator – The central god in the pantheon this world worships. The Creator is a mysterious being who rules over this world from detached indifference. He is responsible for creating everything the eye can see—from the world we live on to the stars in the sky. Smitten with righteous superiority, he's cursed the offspring of Dagon and Damon to pay for Solis and Luna's sins.

Dagon – The first ever Lycan this world has seen who is now worshipped by Lycans as a god; Dagon is a child of Solis and Luna's eclipse, and after the Creator learned of their treachery, he cursed Dagon to turn into a wolfish beast whenever the moon is full.

Damon – The first ever Undead this world has seen who is now worshipped by the Undead as a god; Damon is a child of Solis and Luna's eclipse, and after the Creator learned of their treachery, he cursed Damon to never walk in the sunlight again, and also to forever thirst for the taste of blood.

Luna – The name of the moon and the goddess of night; Luna is worshipped by some and feared by many.

Lycan – Man by day, wolfman by night, the Lycans are a truly fearsome creature infected with an inability to control the beast that dwells within. The full moon calls to the monster inside them, and they are powerless to keep it at bay.

Solis – The name of the sun and the god of the day; Solis turns Undead to ash and provides comfort to Lycans.

Sylvians – A royal family whose bloodline stretches back to the creation of mankind. Known best for their iconic silver eyes, Sylvians are the world's only Undead-Lycan hybrid, and because these curses cancel out in their bodies, they have the ability to call on the powers of both the Undead and the Lycan while retaining full autonomy.

Sylvian the First – After Dagon and Damon were cursed by the Creator, Luna and Solis eclipsed a third time, thus creating Sylvian the First. In him, he possessed both curses his elder brothers suffered from, but in him, these curses cancelled out. Sylvian is worshipped as the god who brought order to earth's people, and it's his offspring who have forever ruled over the kingdom he built.

Undead – Characterized by their purple eyes and silver hair, the Undead are this world's version of vampires.

Trigger Warnings

This story contains potentially disturbing or offensive content that may be harmful to some readers. Examples of this include:

Sexual Assault

Rape

Blood and gore

Extreme violence and death

Death

Grief/Loss

INTRODUCTION

I will keep this short and sweet, seeing I myself skip most introductions when I'm reading books.

"Huntress" was a project I felt called to write on a mere whim.

After a cohort of readers found my first book, "Bloodlust," on TikTok, I received several comments on videos communicating that people wanted to support me but didn't have the money to do so.

As an author who once worked two jobs and still struggled to make ends meet, I never want finances to be what stands between the stories I write and those who want to read them.

That is why I set out to write my first novella and make it completely free to the masses.

The universe I established in "Bloodlust" is one I plan on scaling over the course of my life, and "Huntress" is my first addition to this world of characters who live rent free in my head every day. It serves as a prelude to "Bloodlust," taking place approximately forty years before the events of my debut novel. I did that intentionally, because I didn't want to require readers to buy "Bloodlust" in order to understand this plot.

This story can stand on its own two feet, but many of these characters will live on to make appearances in future novels I release. So, if you grow attached to any of them, rest assured... You will see them again very soon.

1

JOIN, OR DIE

"A draft?" Bogdon questions. "What do you mean there's a draft?"

"Come quick! They're posting it in town square! Knights from the Areopagus itself! Can you believe it? Knights!"

"Knights have never come to Fyrefell," Chloe disputes.

"Drakini," Myre whispers in an urgent tone. My eyes gravitate to him, unsure what to believe at this point. In all my life, nothing this exciting has happened. In my life, nothing this terrifying has happened.

Myre continues, "It's gotta be a misunderstanding... right?" He looks to me for reassurance. I have little to give him.

Seconds ago, I was caught in a daydream while we walked back from the reservoir. My neck and shoulders are tight from balancing the bucket atop my head for several miles. This news was so unsettling to Myre that he dropped his pail and lost several hours worth of hard labor. He's always been an anxious child; the fruits of his labor are now swallowed up by the ashen ground, leaving only a shadow of darkness as they disappear beneath the earth.

I am less foolish. I carefully remove the pail from my head and lower it steadily to the ground, ensuring not a single drop is sacrificed in the commotion.

We just returned to Fyrefell, but there will be no reprieve from our journey. Townsfolk run as if an enemy approaches on the horizon, even though we are guaranteed protection as a fief under the Areopagus Charter. But its the same knights sworn to protect us that visit our peaceful town, so why do citizens run around like we are in danger?

"I'm sure it's just a big misunderstanding," I reply optimistically, hiding the uncertainty in my voice. I am reluctant to leave my water behind, the strain in my muscles a constant reminder of how much work it took to retrieve it, but if Bogdon's words can be trusted, I have much more to worry about than a little dehydration.

I follow the flooding townspeople into town square. Myre clings to my side like a frightened little brother, though he is actually a few months older than me. Chloe and Bogdon are swallowed by the crowd as we approach. People of all ages are gathered. I haven't seen this many Fyrefellians assembled in one place in my entire life. We are a small village, but unity has never been one of our strong suits.

I hear a shrill voice cry out from the front of the crowd, "But what if we don't want to join the child king's army?"

I am not tall enough to see over the looming bodies, but I hear a cold, merciless voice reply. "The choice is yours. Join, or die."

The villagers around me erupt with madness. Voices shout out with unintelligible slurs. The words become lost in the heat of delusion. A few threats rise from the smog of shouting to be heard above the rest.

"They can't kill us all!"

"We didn't sign up for this war!"

"Death to the tyrant!"

"Overthrow the child king!"

Myre grips my arm. I don't bother looking at him. He has been afraid of the world his entire life, but now that the world has validated his fear, he will come undone. I pull my arm from him and push forward through the crowd, only able to hear his shouting for a split second before it's overcome by the raging riot.

The perks of being a teenage female, if any, is my size. I am easily small enough to wade through the townsfolk without pushing or shoving. My body easily conforms to the gaps between individuals and passes through them like water through the cracks of a ravine. I arrive close to the front by the time the initial rage passes and the shouting dies down. Now I can see the brigade of knights that stands posted outside the sheriff's office.

My initial impression of them isn't fear—it is amazement.

All I've ever known is Fyrefell, the small town of ash several miles from Cardone's corpse. Life here has been peaceful, not because we have no enemies, but because people do not travel this sector of the country. Fire mountains surround us, slumbering eons at a time so we are protected from their fire-that-burns-all.

Only knowing Fyrefell has been a quaint experience. But again, I only know Fyrefell. The world outside these ashy plains is unknown to me. Seeing these knights awakens something inside me—something I didn't know was there.

As I peer at their travel-worn armor, I realize there is a whole world out there I haven't seen. Places I convinced myself I cannot go, because I am a teenage girl from a village no one has ever heard of. There are several dozen of them, though I only know how to count as high as a dozen. Each warrior in their band wears a different mix of armor. Some, like their leader, are covered head to toe in it. Others opt for a simple breastplate, gauntlet, and greaves. Those who wear no helm still reveal no emotions on their faces. The soot of our ashen town covers their cheeks and foreheads. They are a merciless group. Killers through and through. The sort of men who take no pity on simpletons like us.

Join, or die, the knight said. I have no idea why the Areopagus has a need for soldiers, but I do know one thing. This draft is my ticket out of here. An opportunity to see the world. A chance to be more than my birth.

The air echoes as a rock bounces off the lead knight's armor. I gasp inwardly, pulled from my daydream. The emotionless tank of armor turns to a man in the crowd that rears back his arm again, then lets a second stone fly. People shrink back in fear as the rock hits its target.

The knight's gaze is cold. His body doesn't even flinch at the attack. The stone doesn't so much as move him. His gray gauntlet reaches to his waist and retrieves a sword from its scabbard. The weapon is an unholy thing, still stained with flecks of dried blood from another place and time.

Quickly, without so much as a word spoken, the knight walks over to the man and thrusts the sword into the rock-thrower's belly, picking him off his feet and lifting him into the air. The Fyrefellian gasps as his body's weight rests against the hilt. He coughs blood onto the knight's helm.

"Insubordination is punishable by death," the knight preaches, teaching his lesson to the crowd the hard way. No one in the crowd speaks as the knight's soldiers all reach for their pommels in anticipation of retaliation. The knight removes his sword from the rock-thrower's stomach and lets the dying man fall to the ashen ground.

"All citizens, men and women, over the age of thirteen and under the age of twenty, are subject to this draft," the knight repeats. This is the central message for their visit. A military draft. Men and women. Over the age of thirteen. Under the age of twenty.

I am sixteen, I think to myself, smiling at the epiphany. I am the only one in the crowd who smiles. Everyone else stares at the rock-thrower's dead body, then stares at the invincible brigade of knights.

The knight continues, "In three day's time you will report to the Areopagus for assessment, training, and assignment. Failure to report will be punishable by death. King Silenius thanks you for your loyalty to the kingdom. Long live the king."

A WOMAN IN A WORLD OF MEN

"**Y**ou aren't going," father says, shattering my dreams before they can even begin.

"You heard the knight, dad!" I shout across our destitute hut. "Insubor-" I stumble over the word, unable to remember its pronunciation and unsure of its meaning in the first place. "Insub... Fek, whatever the word is, it's punishable by death!"

"You're sixteen, Drakini," he yells back. "You know nothing about this world. There's a reason your mother and I stayed in Fyrefell! Have you ever thought about that? We are safe here. Safe from a million and one things you don't even know exist."

"And that safety is not guaranteed, why else would they announce a draft?" I counter, trying to gain logical footing in any way possible.

"It doesn't concern us regardless, Drakini. Human, Lycan, Undead, doesn't matter. No enemy of the Areopagus Throne will travel this close to Cardone. People still think ghosts and demons rule these lands. We are safe from any attack that threatens the kingdom."

"Rumors of ghosts won't protect us forever, dad. They did little to protect mom from bandits when they came to town."

My vision goes blurry as my head is struck by dad's backhand. My ears ring. The floor does little to cushion my fall. Father shouts, "Mention your mother's memory again and…" The ringing in my ear makes it hard to focus on his words. The world is spinning. My eardrums vibrate violently. I am nauseous. My stomach lifts toward my throat. It isn't until I'm lying on the ground that I realize my own father slapped me. His threatening figure looms above me. How did he cross the hut so fast? I didn't even see the strike coming.

I feel powerless. Weak. My head hurts so much I can barely formulate thoughts. My own father. The man who is supposed to love and care for me. Hit me. He hit me. Why? I can't remember. What did I do to deserve this? Surely I must have done something. But I can't remember. My mind is blank. Still, he looms over me and speaks over the ringing.

"This is what waits for you in the draft, Drakini. Pain. You have been sheltered your whole life because I've protected you. You are a woman in a world of men, Drakini. If you think my slap hurts, you have another thing coming. Wait until it's a sword that strikes you, or an arrow, or a whip. Men are strong. Women are weak. It's the way the gods made us. If you join this draft, you will die before you ever see war. Men will put you in the dust and trample over you.

"And that is just the men. The Undead will do worse. They will feed on your blood until you are too weak to stand. They will leave you for the Lycans to pick your body apart like jackals. The king is a child. He is younger than you. He doesn't know the cost of war, and he doesn't care about the soldiers who die. If you leave, you will die. If you leave, there will be no burial for your bones. If you leave, the gods will take the only remembrance I have left of your mother."

His words enter one ear and quickly exit the other. I can't focus. I'm filled with the uncontrollable urge to lay here forever. So I do. When father walks away, I stay on the ground, cushioning my head with my arms. I will sleep here for the night, because the thought of getting up and moving to my bed is too great a burden to bear.

I will submit to my father's wishes. I am too weak to defy his rules. I don't know why I thought I could be a soldier. I am too weak to be a soldier. I am a woman in a world of men. War is not my place.

As I lay on the cold dirt of our hut, I'm suddenly reminded of the pail of water I failed to retrieve. That was our water for this week. I hope no one has stolen it. As the woman of the house, it is my job to make sure we have drinking water. If someone stole the pail, I will have to get more. But I am too weak to make that journey again. Too weak to do even the duties required of me.

I am woman.

I am weak.

I will stay in Fyrefell.

Only here will I be safe.

LACK OF FEISTINESS

I was the only child my age that defied the draft. My father's fear of losing me held me back. The sting in my head taught me I'm not strong enough to disobey his command. I had fallen in line with his every order. I remained when my friends left. Myre, Bogdon, Chloe. Fonz, Lily, Kirk. They had all left, whether they wanted to or not. They all marched for Areopagus to report for their duties, none of them looking back.

Father and I remained, tending to our daily chores, ignoring the silence that filled Fyrefell in the absence of so many. This town was no longer the same as it was. No laughing, no joy. Just those who've had their loved ones stolen for a war they didn't start.

I was an empty husk after being knocked unconscious by my own father, the only man in this world who was supposed to love me unconditionally. The world was no longer colorful to my eyes. It was a dull gray devoid of positive emotions. What's worse was the speculation of what would happen if I actually went to war. If dad was able to hurt me so bad, and he loves me, then what would someone who hated me do?

The question was chilling to consider.

But everything changed when the knights came back to town.

Seven days was all it took for the king's army to learn of our absence. Seven days, then they came for us.

The memory is hazy, probably because I've done my best to pretend it never happened. I just remember the knocking of metal knuckles on our hut's door, followed by it being kicked in like it was nothing more than thin glass. Father shouted, attempting to do to these knights what he did to me.

But the knights were not the same as a defenseless teenage girl, and it turns out father is not as strong as I made him out to be.

I remember blood, lots of blood.

I didn't know a human body had so much blood. It's nearly endless.

And I can remember my screams echoing off the walls as I protested the massacre, too scared to join my father in defiance. I can't remember how many of them there were. I just remember the feeling of my clothes being ripped from my body. The feeling of being powerless.

One after the other, the knights took me for their own sadistic pleasures. They spread my legs and deflowered me, then flipped me on my stomach and thrust until my lower half went numb. I stopped screaming after I realized no one was coming to my aid. My vocal chords snapped in two. I suffered in silence, letting them have their way with me, clutching the dirt beneath me with my fists, pretending it was just one big nightmare.

Father was right. Men are strong. Women are weak. It's the way the gods made us. Not all men are created equal though, and father was not strong enough to protect me from this attack. In this sense, I too was right.

Dad wasn't strong enough to protect mom from being raped and killed by bandits. Ever since then, it was his world that was devoid of color. He never recovered from the trauma of losing mom, and I learned to not bring up her memory for fear of provoking him.

I stared at his bloodied corpse as the knights degraded me. Some were kinder than the others. Others were more abusive than some. My hair ripped from my scalp where they pulled at it. My flesh bruised like a peach where they held me down. I learned quickly to not squirm. It only made them frustrated, and they took their frustrations out on me.

For the duration of my raping, it wasn't the rape that scared me, but the uncertainty of what would happen afterwards. Would they kill me like they did my father? Were those to be my final moments on this earth, my genitals a sacrifice to their unrelenting seed?

No, that's not how I'll be remembered.

I remember seeing a dagger on one of their hips. I don't know how, but it ended up in my grip. I remember blood splattering onto my face from my assailant's throat. Some of it got in my mouth, burning my hoarse throat as it went down. His body went limp atop me, bathing me as he bled out. His body was heavy, but his plated armor was heavier. It pinned me to the ground as I reached around his body and drove the dagger into his back repeatedly, screaming silently because my throat was broken.

"Maybe there's a place for this one in our forces after all," one laughed. "Gods know the women never make it for lack of feistiness."

I don't remember what happened next. I felt a force knock me unconscious, this one much more powerful than my father's slap. My brain was already fractured, but this blow shattered it altogether. Normally unconsciousness protected me from the world of pain, but not that time. That time, the pain followed me into the darkness, and in the darkness, I could still feel the hands of several knights holding me down as my body shook from their thrusts.

4

STICKBALL

"You will not be judged for what is in between your legs, but for how you can swing a sword," the Arms Master shouts. "So get up, damn woman, and stop feeling sorry for yourself!"

There is not enough oxygen in the atmosphere for me to catch my breath. My lungs are not on fire, they *are* fire. It feels as if I'm breathing steam through a bamboo straw. My wheezing is the only thing I can hear. That, and the incessant ringing in my ears from my battered brain.

The sunlight makes it painful to look at my surroundings. It feels as though my eyeballs have been stabbed, as if someone is trying to push them out of my sockets. The pressure is unbearable. I just want the pain to go away, but the Arms Master finds sick pleasure in watching me be thrown to the ground.

I look at my opponent. He is much bigger than me, much bigger than other males I've faced. After being forcefully removed from my home in

Fyrefell, my oppressors brought me straight to Areopagus like a fugitive. I have been dropped straight into the pool of draftees; we are being assessed on our abilities to fight and kill. These trials are not meant to teach us how to fight, but to assess our raw talent in the sport of killing.

Everything we do is being watched and scored. Anonymous commanders from numerous military sects sit elevated above the drilling fields. It is like open tryouts, though none of us know what teams we are competing for. Our instructions are simple. Fight like hell, because our entire military career hangs in the balance.

I've yet to win a fight thus far. The deck has been stacked against me since my arrival. I have seven days less training than my opponents. My body is still broken and bruised from my raping. The space between my legs is tender to the touch, making every step I take a painful reminder of my inferiority. My head feels like dead wood consumed by termites. It has been scrambled like eggs from being struck over and over.

I stand back to my feet, heaving my oversized sword and shield. They are too heavy for me, designed for a man to wield. I stare at my opponent. He twirls his sword whimsically, waiting for me to get my shit together before attacking again. I am not going to win this fight going blade to blade. My arms burn just from holding the sword and shield, and it takes entirely too much momentum to swing them.

Drop them, a voice whispers from beside me. I look to my right and nearly fall back to my bruised ass. The sword and shield fall from my grip, not because I obey the monster's command, but because I am so startled from its presence.

What the fuck is happening?

My weapons kick up dust at the feet of the hellcat. The petite beast stares up at me, eyeing me with a feral glare. *Trust me, I am here to help you*, it speaks. I look around, confused where the beast came from. I have never seen an animal that resembles this creature before. It is like a mix between a lynx and a panther, black as night with a shaggy mane that swoops into a closely-cropped beard. Two fangs descend from the roof of its mouth like curved daggers.

"What the fuck are you?" I ask aloud, confused how this monster is able to communicate with me.

"Yield, Drakini!" My opponent shouts, "I find no pleasure beating on a woman, but I have no choice but to put you down if you keep standing back up!"

I am going to help you defeat him, the hellcat says. I look around, wondering if anyone else sees the monster by my side. The Arms Master's face is indifferent, and my opponent doesn't reveal any surprise at the appearance of this beast. *They can't see me, if that's what you're wondering. Only you can see me*, it answers the question I seek for.

"But why?"

Because you are Worthy, Huntress.

"What the hell are you talking about?"

Take out your dagger.

I don't know why, but I comply. I draw the shortened blade from the scabbard on my hip, unsure what it will do to protect me from my formidable opponent. It causes him to laugh from across the barren battlefield. His laugh hurts my eardrums. I clench the dagger's hilt tight as I try to block out his mockery.

"What can I do with this? He will cut me in half if I charge him without a shield."

Who said anything about charging? the hellcat asks, purring violently. *This world has not been fair to you, so it's time to even the playing field. I want you to take aim and throw it.*

"You want me to what?" I ask, blood freezing in my veins. I stare back at my opponent. He is covered from head to toe in armor. He stands two heads taller than me. The sword and shield in his grip look like extensions of his own body. Five times he's slung me to the ground, barely making an effort to fight me, a woman vastly inferior to him.

The more I think of it, the more I realize he's been showing me kindness this entire fight. He could have killed me by now, or knocked me unconscious as my other opponents have. But instead he's given me opportunity after opportunity to yield, something no one else has offered me.

So why have I kept getting back up and persisting on fighting? I have nothing to prove, I already know I am the weaker of us two.

Remember when you used to play stickball as a child?

"How do you know about stickball?" The memory is not one anyone would know except fellow village children.

They would always make you play pitcher, because you had the fastest throw, the hellcat replies, not acknowledging my question. *It is just like that. Throw the dagger fast. Let its weight do the rest.*

I rear the dagger back, pinching the blade between my index finger and thumb. My eyes lock onto my target. I see a noticeable gap in my opponent's armor between his breastplate and shoulder guard. If I can manage to hit him there on his sword arm, it will make it harder for him to swing, and even the playing field between my weakness and his strength.

I channel my anger and fear, then let the dagger fly, twisting my hips and letting the momentum pivot my shoulders. Suddenly, it feels like the dagger is an extension of my body. I connect with it in the same way my adversary bonds with sword and shield. The throwing motion feels natural—it's the same one I've repeated countless times on the stickball field.

I feel bad for my opponent. He doesn't expect me to stoop to such a low level attack, throwing a dagger in a competition of hand-to-hand combat. He isn't even looking at me when the dagger goes airborne. He is eyeing the Arms Master, wondering how much longer he will let this fight go on.

A muffled grunt escapes his lungs as the dagger hits its intended target, severing the ligaments in his vulnerable shoulder as the blade separates everything that holds his arm in socket. His sword drops out of his hand unexpectedly. A look of bewilderment clenches his face. It is like he has been stung by an invisible bee, fearful of when the next attack may come.

The massive foe looks around, trying to figure out where the dagger came from. It's telling that he looks to me last, convinced I am not capable of such a feat. It happened so fast. One moment I was lying defenseless on the ground, the next I've delivered a debilitating blow. The Arms Master's jaw drops as my opponent's sword thuds to the ground. A chill of joy passes through me like lightning.

What is this feeling inside me? Is that pride? No, I realize... That's power.

Good shot, the hellcat purrs. *Now, charge him.*

The feeling fades as quick as it rose. "I can't do that... He will destroy me."

No, my darling. He won't even land a single blow.

"Yeah, because he will land several," I joke nervously. The hellcat doesn't find my humor amusing.

If you want my help, you will listen to me. I have no time for those who don't trust me.

I go to pick up my sword but am stopped. The hellcat growls at me, then pounces on the sword to prevent me from picking it up. *No sword!*

"I have no other weapons," I stammer.

You need no weapons to defeat this man. Believe in yourself, darling.

Against my better judgment, I charge my adversary, so nervous I could vomit. He eyes me fearfully, reaching with his shield hand to pull the blade from his opposite shoulder. This is not the simple matchup it was thirty seconds ago. I've drawn blood, proving myself worthy.

Dante rips the dagger from his shoulder and staggers his feet, one arm hanging limp at his side. He drops his shield and picks up his sword with his nondominant hand, twirling it awkwardly like it is a foreign object.

I wonder what goes through his head as I close the distance between us. Seconds ago, he begged me to yield. Five times he put me in the dirt. Six times I got back up. I don't know why I refuse to quit. It's like I know I'm weaker, and that realization frustrates me past the point of giving up.

Maybe, just maybe, if I refuse to concede, my determination will make up for my inferiority.

"Don't do this," he mouths silently to me, shaking his head as he readies his next strike.

Do this, the hellcat growls, running beside me.

My feet kicks up the dust of the clay field we spar on as I come within striking distance of him. Dante swings.

Everything slows, literally. My vision tunnels on the arc of the sword. Why is it moving so slow? It's like he's cutting through gelatin on his way to reach me. More than that, his body is slow, like it's moving through water. But my speed remains the same, though the thought of it seems impossible.

Reality itself distends to slow time. I'm able to track his sword's swing moment by lurching moment. I duck under the swing, bringing me in close to his body. I spin around him and leap on his exposed back, his body off balance from the half-hearted strike. It is the perfect storm. His lack of balance, my momentum, his sluggishness, my speed. I wrap the inside of my elbow around his trachea and push the back of his head into the chokehold, cutting off his supply of air. The sword arc follows through, missing its target by embarrassing margins.

He panics, dropping his sword to remove the vice grip I exert over him. I can feel the beat of his heart through his thick neck. It does all it can to supply his brain with oxygenated blood. It is the same tactic I used on village kids when they used to pick fights with Myre. Back when I was the only one strong enough to defend him—back when I was still confident in my own abilities.

My father took away my confidence. The knights stripped me of my self-worth. But now, in this moment, all of that disappears. The pain. The inferiority. The shame.

Suddenly, I am the girl I used to be. The one who didn't fear the world or the unknown. The girl who smiled when she got a black eye from fights with other children. The stickball player who spit blood when a stray pitch knocked a tooth from her mouth. The tomboy who went toe to toe with bigger and stronger children just for the thrill of it.

Dante drops to his knees, then falls flat on his face, unconscious. I collapse atop of him, panting, exhausted. I roll off his armor and stare up at the sky, a smile on my face for the first time in a long time.

I won, I realize. For the first time in a long time, I won.

I sit up and turn to thank the hellcat but find no such companion. She has vanished, leaving me to cherish the victory I wouldn't have won without her.

"Victor, Drakini," Arms Master announces to the military scouts above. I look up at them, sitting in a shaded portion of the amphitheater, scribbling notes on pads regarding our performance. The sun strikes my eyes as I look up at them, forcing me to lower my head back to the ground. Still, I smile.

My body and brain may hurt, but the pain has less sting knowing I won.

5

DODGEBALL

"Fight!" Arms Master shouts, moving out of the way and off to the side of the fighting field.

"Where the fuck are you?" I mumble under my breath, looking around for the hellcat. It has been almost the full span of a day since my victory over Dante, and the Lynx-like ally has yet to reappear. I had so many questions to ask it, but now that I am back on the fighting grounds, all I care about is having its direction so I don't get the shit belliwhopped out of me.

My adversary this round is female, like myself, but I won't underestimate her. I have heard terrible things about this woman. Rumors spread around the barracks faster than lice from cot to cot. Before any given match, I know just enough about my opponent to fill my stomach with reverent nausea.

We each have seven fights under our belts, all of which were exhibition and meant little. But the fights we've won or lost up until today make up our record, which establishes our ranking going into the tournament.

What we fight for now has much more at stake. Winners advance; losers go to recruiting.

From my understanding, you must make it several days into the tournament before your prospects of recruitment increase. Those knocked out of the tournament the first few days will be picked up by infantry. I am just a girl from Fyrefell without knowledge of the military, but the other children my age talk about the infantry as if it's a death sentence. They are the front lines in war. Minimally trained and highly expendable. With only a few days worth of fighting under their belts, fighters knocked from the tournament have little to show on their scorecards. The more elite branches of the military are less likely to risk a recruitment slot for someone who isn't worth their own salt.

The rules are simple—simple elimination, winner advances. Yield and I lose. Be knocked unconscious and I lose. Sustain life threatening injury and I lose. Die and... Well, I lose.

We are ranked in groups by the thousand, and I am Number 879. Not dead last, but certainly not in the upper half. With only one win separating me from having six losses, I have little confidence in my own abilities. The lower half of the bracket is matched against the upper half. The 1000th slot is pitted against the 1st, the 999th against the 2nd, and on and on. It makes sense to me—why pit the lower half against each other when the recruiters are really here to see the upper half put their skills to use?

The female standing on the other side of the fighting field is Number 121. Nowhere near Number 1, but she only has one loss out of seven thus far, and as far as I'm concerned, that's a helluva lot better than me. Kendra is her name, but the people in my barracks call her Slingshot, after her less-than-normal weapon of choice. Few who have faced her have closed the distance between them. In her hand is nothing more than a leather sling held together by two strings. At her waist is a bag filled with small, dense rocks.

I have heard of the sling before, but I didn't know it was useful for fighting. Local shepherds in Fyrefell trained themselves to be deadly accurate with the sling, but their target was always predators that endangered their flock. Coyotes and vultures and mountain lions, mainly. I have seen the devastation such a weapon can enact by nothing more than a rock and forward momentum. Orso, my father's friend who tended sheep, once carried a coyote over his shoulder to our house to show my father. As a little girl, my whole fist could fit in the hole that cracked its skull from the rock's entry.

Facing such a weapon in Kendra's hands, I know yielding is not an option. If I am hit by one of her strikes, I could very well die before I register I've been hit.

I rub my sweaty fingers across my palms, then reach for my twin daggers. I, too, have opted for a less conventional weapon than sword and shield. If it isn't broke, there is no need to fix it. I lost six battles with sword and shield in my hands. I am undefeated from the moment I picked up the dagger.

But I know the truth of the matter—my dagger has nothing to do with my victory and everything to do with the hellcat. Where she came from, I have no idea. Where she went, I am clueless. Why I am the only one who saw her, well... I think I know the answer to that one. I am going insane.

Mother was the same way, before the bandits got her. Said she saw spirits during the day and demons at night. Sometimes I would catch her talking to them, as if they were visitors to our home. The delusions were worse some days and nonexistent others. I caught her setting a dinner plate for someone that was imaginary once, and another time in an argument with someone that wasn't there. It was like watching her scream at a wall, which frightened me as a child. But as I grew older, it was my new normal.

Mom spoke to things that weren't there. It became as normal as water being wet and fire being hot.

The more I think about the hellcat, the more I'm convinced I am seeing things that aren't actually there. It is the only way to make sense of it. Dante said nothing about the hellcat, and neither did the Arms Master. Yet the animal seemed as real as the intricate fingerprints on my palms. But it could talk...

"Focus," I tell myself, tightening my grip on the daggers. I can't lose this fight. I must advance. I have proved myself. My father's slap doesn't define me. My raping doesn't mean shit. I was wrong to let them infect my mind. They are tumorous memories, and I must cut them away. Free myself from my past so I can define my own future.

And that future begins here, by putting Kendra in the dirt.

I stalk toward my foe slowly, like a hellcat would. Something has changed in me since my last battle. My feet move with instinctual confidence. My fear dissipates. The anticipation anxiety I felt this morning drains from my body. I am here. My objective is simple. I must get Kendra to yield, or I must hurt her so badly that she cannot go on.

Kendra loads her first stone and eyes me arrogantly. She has six wins. Six times she's slung that sling and hit her target with enough damage to be called victor. Her luck ends with me. I won't make this easy for her. If she's to hit me, I'll make her do it while I'm on the move.

I move from side to side, never remaining in the same place for longer than a half second, every step bringing me closer to her. Sometimes I'll take two steps to the same side, then fake a change of direction. This is a mind game. She needs to aim where she thinks I'll be, not where I am now.

She lifts the sling and begins twirling. My feet can't fail me now. I can feel her eyes locking onto me like a tyrfalcon on a field mouse. My daggers are ready. If she misses me, it will be the end of her. I haven't slept since my fight with Dante. I spent all night in the practice yard, throwing daggers at target dummies. I have committed myself to these weapons. Hitting Dante may have been dumb luck, but hitting Kendra won't be. The muscle memory from my stickball pitching days saved me last fight, but I've seared the memory back into my muscles, adjusting from throwing a ball to throwing blades.

The sling picks up speed. I need to anticipate its release. I need to make Kendra aim where she thinks I'll be, and I need to not be there when the stone arrives.

I slide left, left, fake right, then left.

My vision distorts and my body hits the ground. A ringing emerges in my ear as everything goes blurry. I don't even feel the ground catch me as I fall.

The world spins violently. I am falling from the sky with nothing to slow my descent. The ringing is so loud I fear my brain may explode. My body is convulsing uncontrollably. Foam and spit froth at my mouth. The sun blinds me. Everything is white. I can't see. I'm panicking, but I can't move voluntarily. My body is controlled by the spastic movements of my seizing muscles.

A shadow descends on me, blocking out the sun. Still, my vision is too blurry to perceive the outside world.

Get up, a voice purrs over the ringing. Somehow, the voice puts me at ease. My body goes still. I swallow the foam in my mouth. The ringing subsides. I can't explain it. One moment, it felt as if I was dying, on my way to heaven's gates. The next, I am back on the ground, perfectly fine.

I sit up, dazed and confused. "Where am I?" I whisper, looking around. The first thing I see is the hellcat beside me, its shadow shielding my eyes from the merciless sun above. I am sitting on the battlefield, I realize. I don't remember getting here. I don't remember waking up this morning.

Wait a second, I reflect on my memories. I don't remember waking up because I never slept. I spent all night in the practice yards, throwing daggers at target dummies. The memories are coming back to me in small handfuls. Still though, I don't remember entering the tournament for my fight, nor do I remember who I'm supposed to be fighting. I look up and see a woman on the other side of the field. The Arms Master is raising her hand to declare victory. She's looking at me with a dumbfounded look, as if she's never seen someone sit on the battlefield before. It causes me further confusion. Why am I sitting, I ask myself. The woman taps the Arms Master on the shoulder, then points at me.

Arms Master Garmin Vaid turns to face me, then lowers Kendra's arm. He too is confused. I rub my temple, a migraine building behind my eyes. My forehead is slick with blood and is bitterly painful to the touch.

"Drakini of Fyrefell, do you yield?" Garmin asks. Why would he ask that? The fight hasn't even started yet, nor do I remember how I got here. It's a stupid question to ask, as if I'd just give up this fight without trying my hand for a chance to advance in the tournament. Do these recruiters just want me to roll over and be sent to infantry? I may only have a record of one win and five losses, but I am still a fighter.

I look to the hellcat. "Where have you been?"

I arise from necessity, and you didn't need me until now, she answers. *Now get up, you're embarrassing me.*

I rise to my feet and collect my daggers from the dusty ground. I am clueless how they got there, but that is the least of my worries. Blood drips from my temple into my eye. I wipe it away like a tear, but more flows to replace it. What in the world is happening? It feels like my body's been hit by a bull and trampled by its hooves. And my head is spinning, causing me to stagger a few steps until I gain balance.

"Did someone fucking drug me and drag me out here?"

No, much worse, the hellcat purrs. *Your face just ate a shot from Slingshot girl over there. Frankly, it was embarrassing to watch.*

"I don't even remember the fight starting, let alone being hit by a stone."

Exactly. That's kind of the point.

"Touché," I reply, passively relieved by the hellcat's explanation.

Your memory will come back, but your pride won't.

"Alright, alright, that's enough ridicule."

I will slow down time for you again so you can dodge her next shot, but seriously, you need to protect your head. You're about two hits past having soup between your ears.

"Slow down time? Like you did so I could best Dante?"

Time is a perception of the mind, and I was born from the cracks in your brain. I can alter your perceptions so the world around you is what I deem fit.

"Cracks in the brain?" I stutter, unsure what the hellcat means.

Is this really a conversation you want to have now? Your opponent has already loaded the next stone.

"Drakini, answer me!" Garmin Vaid yells out once more. "Do you yield?"

"Now why on earth would I do that?" I scream back. "This fight is just getting started!"

That's my girl, the hellcat purrs.

"Don't slow time," I order, "I can handle this now."

Stickball isn't the only game I'm used to playing. As a kid, we would also play dodgeball, a game where you throw balls at one another and are taken out of the game if hit. Kids are devious, and so am I. I developed a strategy early on to ensure I could hit other kids with my throws. Distract them long enough on one thing and they won't even see you throwing a fatal pitch.

I would throw one ball easy enough for them to dodge and get their attention fixated on avoiding it, then, right when they were reassured they wouldn't be hit, I would throw a second ball, this time as fast and accurate as I could manage. With my pitching abilities, it was always a sure fire way to get someone out.

I do the same now, twirling my daggers in my hands. I am only a few dozen feet from Kendra as she begins spinning her sling above her head. I won't let her get off a second shot.

I rear back my dominant hand and let the dagger fly, purposefully throwing it slow and off target. Kendra's eyes lock onto it, accepting the bait I've spoon fed her. How could winning be this easy? This woman is ranked Number 121, but she doesn't act like it. No sweat off my back. While the first dagger has only made it halfway to its target, I switch my other blade into my dominant hand and rear back, eyeing Kendra's movement. She steps to her right, a smile on her face as she judges my first throw. Her arrogance will be the end of her.

I put my whole body into the second throw, yeeting the dagger as hard as I can manage, flicking my wrist like I practiced all night. It is a perfect throw, and Kendra doesn't even see it coming. The first dagger flies right by her, wide left. I love seeing the smile on her arrogant face. I love even more watching it disappear as my second throw buries itself into the wrist that holds her sling. I hope she knows that's exactly what I was aiming for for two reasons. First, because I am a kind woman, and I would not aim for a killing blow against someone who isn't my real enemy. And second, because I want her to know how deadly accurate I am with these blades. A bitch's skinny wrist is a helluva lot smaller of a target than her male-width broad shoulders.

She screams. The sling flies from her grip. Her forearm is split in two by the dagger, severing the ligaments necessary so she can do nothing other than hold her hand open like she's waving at me. Now I am the one that smiles, and I sprint to close the gap while she is in dismay. Kendra is not concerned with where I am, all she can manage to do is stare at her wrist like her hand's grown an extra finger. Dramatic bitch, I scoff. What would she have done if I aimed for her sternum instead?

Kendra sees me too late. I jump in the air, my kneecap raised and flying for her face. She may have six wins, but they are all from hitting her opponent with her slingshot. I can tell from her frightened gaze she has no proficiency in hand-to-hand combat. She screams, "I yiel-"

Too late. My knee reaches her nose before she can get the surrender out, and I feel the bones in her face crack as my body weight carries the strike through her. She collapses on the ground like a bag of potatoes. I look up to the shadowy spectator stands and see the recruiters in the top row, heads buried in their notes as they scribble furiously. "Victor, Drakini of Fyrefell!" Garmin shouts, running over to me. I let him raise my arm ceremoniously, then rip my dagger from Kendra's unconscious body. Tomorrow, she will be picked up by the infantry and trained for the front lines—a place where they have no need for slingshot shooters; a place where she will die and few will remember her name.

6

SAME SIDE

"Drakini of Fyrefell," a messenger calls into the barracks.

"That's me," I reply, unused to hearing my name be pronounced so formally.

"Arms Master Garmin Vaid calls for you. You can locate him in the Forge. That is all," the messenger says, leaving the barracks as fast as he entered. I look around, and those who heard the message scowl at me. The barracks are emptier than I'm used to. Yesterday, there were one thousand of us. Today, there are only five hundred. Tomorrow, two-hundred and fifty. And on and on until there only remains one, champion of the draft's tournament. The losers of yesterday's matches are no longer here. They have been shipped off for recruiting, most of them praying someone will want them other than infantry.

We who remain are not friends. We are warriors forced to share the same space and tolerate each other's existence. There is no privacy in the barracks. It is a long building made of concrete slabs erected in a rectangular prism. Cots are packed as close to one another as manageable and the only area we have for ourselves is our footlocker, where our meager possessions are stored.

I make the walk of shame from my cot to the barrack's exit doors, feeling the weight of several hundred eyes burning into my back. Though we aren't supposed to talk about our wins and losses, these people seem to know I am one of the few underdogs that survived to today. The bottom half of the 1,000 wasn't supposed to survive yesterday, so they look at me like I'm some sort of cheater.

I don't know what crawled up their asses, Wisteria growls. *You'd think they'd be excited to fight against a weakling like you.*

"Ouch," I grumble under my breath to the hellcat prancing at my side. "I think they know I bested Dante two days ago. He's projected to be one of the tournament's finalists, and I'm his only loss so far."

The big oaf that caught your dagger with his armpit? Wisteria laughs. *That's the best fighter this draft will produce?*

"You're quite the peach today, Wisteria. What's got you in such a mood?"

We have better things to be doing than talking to the Arms Master. You should be training now. Your next fight will not be any easier. They don't like that you won yesterday. Whoever organizes these fights will seek to put you out of your misery.

"I trained all night. I haven't slept in two days. What more can I do to become stronger?"

You can throw a dagger, yes, but what will you do when you need to use them in combat? Hmm? Can you stop a sword's downward arc from splitting you in two with those knives? Can you parry a thrust with those fickle blades? And what happens if you throw both and fail to kill your target? Or miss? You'll be weaponless. There are too many contingencies you haven't trained for.

"Enough," I reply. "I get it. I'm learning on the fly here, hellcat. I haven't even been here for two weeks, and these other kids have seven days of training over me. I've been doing as you've instructed. But with you, I can't lose. You can literally slow time for me. These people can't kill what they can't hit."

Is that enough for you? To be strong because you have me? Will you ever be proud of yourself in life if everything is won leaning on my powers?

"I won the last fight without your help."

Barely, Wisteria purrs. *Your brain is still scrambled eggs from Kendra's slingshot. You're lucky you didn't die. You have only the Creator to thank for making you hard-headed.*

"A win is a win," I dismiss her argument altogether, pushing away the anxiety inside me. She's right, though. I don't feel confident on the battlefield without Wisteria by my side. Part of me feels like an imposter still being in the tournament, and the dirty glares from my adversaries only makes me feel like more of a phony.

Don't worry, I am only being hard on you because I know what's at stake, and because the Creator knows you need some tough love if we're to make you an efficient killer.

I enter the Forge from Areopagus's military sector streets. My body is blasted by a wave of heat as metal rings out all around me. I have been drafted for war, and blacksmiths are required to equip an army. All around me, strong men pound away at the impurities in iron to create weapons of destruction. The Forge is thrice the size of the barracks with only a fraction the manpower.

Everywhere I look are smoldering fires hot enough to melt flesh and bone. The blacksmiths labor over the fires, their skin covered with a sheen of soot and sweat. They pay me no mind as I enter their presence. Their hammers strike away in rhythmic beats. I have no idea what war required this draft, nor do I know my future enemy. All I know is that these blacksmiths take their job seriously, and they will not let us fighters lose for lack of firepower.

"Ah, Drakini!" Garmin calls out, leaving his supervisory post. I have never seen him in a setting like this. Though he has officiated all my fights, Vaid is always well-groomed and freshly bathed on the fighting fields. Now, he is like all the other blacksmiths around me. I barely recognize him under the layer of ash. If it weren't for his familiar voice, I wouldn't even know it was him.

"A messenger said you were calling for me?"

"Yes, yes, thank you for coming. Come, follow me, I made something for you," he says, leading me away from the overstimulating clang of hammers falling in cacophony.

I'm thrown off by the statement as I stumble after him, the heat making me uncomfortable. He made something for me? I barely know this man. I haven't exchanged more than a few words with him on the battlefield, and those words were obligatorily given. His black, short-cropped hair is slicked back with sweat. He wears little clothing under his smithing apron, and his muscles pop from his tight tank top littered with burn holes and stains.

His skin color is lighter than brown but darker than tan, the same color natives of the desert exhibit. His beard, like his hair, is well-groomed, clinging tightly to his jawline as if he shaves it every morning upon waking.

All things considered, he is a handsome man. All things considered, I feel something flutter in my stomach at the thought of him making something for me. This is the first time since my arrival in Areopagus someone has shown me a nicety. Yet he guides me to a table as if this is normal for him, to be showing kindness to someone who didn't ask for it.

"Here, here, gather around," he says. I approach the table and look at what's been laid before me. "I've very much enjoyed watching your fighting style evolve over the past days, but I'm very concerned about your head after yesterday. You were unconscious for almost a minute after being hit by Kendra's slingshot. And you were stumbling when you stood. I fear if you take another hit like that, you won't be getting back up to fight again, so I went to work making this for you."

Garmin lifts a helm off the table and extends it for my inspection. "An unconventional helm to match your unconventional style," he says. My jaw drops as I grab hold of the sleek faceplate. It is like nothing I've seen before, and I've now grown used to seeing knights in armor on a daily basis.

The helm is two separate pieces that separate at the jaw. One is a vented mask made to cover my mouth, nose, and cheek bones, and the other is a rounded plate that can cover from the back of my head to my forehead, cutting off just short of my eyes. The metal itself is sleek and weightless, but when I go to bend it I find that it is too durable to yield to my strength. The only portion of my face that is not covered by these detached plates is the space where my eyes will see, and there is no metal in the way of my peripheral vision.

The inside of the helm is stuffed with cushioning and mesh, and when I slip it over my hair it fits snug enough to remain motionless when I bob my head. I snap the mouthplate in place and breathe through the ventilated mesh. Whatever material fabric he's used, it is thin enough to almost feel like I'm breathing regularly.

I look at Garmin through the opening and see his reaction. He crosses his arms and looks at me in awe. "You look frightening, Drakini of Fyrefell. I would hate to be the one standing opposite of you on the battlefield. What do you think? How does it feel?" I'm speechless. I have no idea what to say to this man. No one, in all my years, has given me something like this. How long did it take him to make? Better yet, why me? Why go out of his way to create something I've done nothing to deserve?

For a brief moment, fear fills me. Does Garmin want something from me? Memories of knights pushing my face in the dirt fill my head. The space between my legs quivers. My heartbeat quickens. I stagger backward, the heat of the Forge making me lightheaded.

Get out of your head, child, Wisteria purrs behind me. *I know what you are thinking, but this is not that kind of man.*

Her words help me snap out of it. The delirium passes over me, burned away by the sweltering heat of smithing fires. I am the iron, and the Forge burns these thoughts of impurity from my mind.

"I have no words to express my gratitude," my voice echoes from within the helm. I don't know what to say, so I speak the exact thoughts on my mind. "Why me? I mean... What did I do to deserve this?"

Garmin dismisses my self-pity with a wave of his hand. "We are not so different, Drakini of Fyrefell. Both Commoners stolen from our villages, both doing our parts to answer King Silenius's calling... Truth be told, this is my job. I am the Arms Master—I exist to aid fighters in combat. What I have done for you today, I would do for anyone. Don't let this tournament hide the truth. We are all on the same side."

"I won't forget this." I open my arms to hug him. He looks down at his oily, ash-covered skin and insists I don't. I pay no mind to him. I have never been afraid of a little sweat and dirt. I wrap my arms around his body and pull him close, tears welling at the thought of having someone in my corner.

Alright, alright, enough of this. We have training to do, Wisteria growls impatiently. *That next fight isn't going to win itself.*

I release Garmin, then unclasp the helm and remove it, taking it with me. He has a smile on his face, almost as if he believes in me. It is a comforting thought. Before today, I believed I was the only person cheering for me.

"Goodluck today, Drakini!" Garmin shouts as I stride off, heading for the Forge's exit and toward the training fields.

Maybe, just maybe, this draft wasn't the worst thing to happen to me.

7

WAR WAITS FOR NO WOMAN

A gain, Wisteria growls, pawing at my back as I lay face down in the dirt. Garmin's helm protected my head from the brutal fall, but my ears still ring nonetheless.

I stand back to my feet, knowing I only have a few short hours before my name will be called for the next round of the tournament. My muscles burn from the incessant drilling. Sweat has soaked the padding inside my helm and now doubles as a cooling mechanism.

Smol gorl weak, Havick grunts, cracking the knuckles of all four arms. *Smol gorl fall easy.*

I stare at my opponent, another monster Wisteria has summoned from my fractured brain to aid me in fighting. I no longer question her methods; the hellcat is the only reason I've survived this far in the tournament, and she's right to make me learn hand-to-hand combat.

Havick may be imaginary, but the pain from his punches is real. *If you can fight a man with four arms, fighting one with two will be easy,* Wisteria had said when Havick appeared from thin air. He stands taller than even Dante, his body laced with the strength of gods. His biceps are bigger than my head; his face is like that of an ogre. He wears no shirt, revealing his whipcord muscles covered with tribal tattoos from his neck to his waist.

The monster's intelligence is lacking, but he makes up for it with brute strength. When he speaks, he does so in a way I hardly understand. Wisteria said she was born from the cracks in my brain, and so was Havick, both arising from necessity. To the outside observer, I must look crazy exchanging blows with thin air and talking to creatures that aren't really here.

But this is my reality, and though these beings may not be real to others, Havick's punches still send me reeling regardless of his visibility to others.

I charge Havick again, throwing myself back into the fray. I will make him regret calling me weak. I steady my breath and focus on the path before me. I slow down time like Wisteria taught me. Time is a construct of the mind, but I need not be bound by it. With the world around me slowed, I can see oncoming attacks long before they reach me. I can dodge them, I can block them, I can counter them, all before their deliverer has time to launch another.

I have no shield, but I no longer have a need for a strong defense. I need no defense if I can dodge every strike. Havick's two right arms cock back and thrust forward, both aimed for my body. They are moving through invisible quicksand to reach me.

I sidestep the double fist collision and send my shin into his hip. His bones are thick, but my shin guards mitigate my pain and worsen his. His right fists fly past me but suddenly change direction. He cocks his elbows in a right angle and throws his elbows in reverse on a collision course for my head.

I leap backward and avoid the blow by a finger's length. That was close. Even though I've slowed his movements to half speed, Havick fights with no remorse. I must be better if I'm to best this troglodyte. I charge again, then slide onto the ground, my upper leg aimed for the inside of Havick's groin. My heel connects with a pressure point and causes Havick to howl. He's furious now. All four of his fists raise in the air and fall on me like hammers on heated metal. I kick off his groin and slide away, spinning so my feet are under me again.

When his fists strike the place my body just was, I use his momentum against him, jumping with my knee raised on course to strike his massive forehead. My feet leave the ground and I'm sailing. After hours of dueling and getting my ass handed to me, I'm finally a half second away from defeating Havick, a figment of my own imagination.

I hold my breath. Time is still moving slow as I float through the air. I curse inwardly. The anticipation is killing me. So close, yet so far.

My breath releases as I feel something grab hold of my straightened leg, ripping my body from its collision course and catapulting me into the ground. My shoulder takes the brunt of the impact, then my head cracks into the ground.

My helm rings out as dirt fills my visor. My body slides across the clay practice yards for several feet and I lay there, defeated.

Somehow, some way, Havick was fast enough to thwart my attack. I hear his deep, guttural laughs booming over me. *I broke smol gorl. She fink Havick slow. I show her. I show her real good, aye Wisteria?*

Yes, good boy, Havick. I think that's all we need for now. Go rest, we will call on you tonight for more training, Wisteria purrs.

I hear him crack all sixteen knuckles before he vanishes from sight as if he never existed in the first place.

Get up, we are needed at the arena. Your name will be called soon.

I roll onto my back and unclasp the helm, the dirt in my visor falling free as I pull it off. My hair falls around me as I wheeze for air. I have never been this exhausted in all my life. All I want is to lay here for the rest of the day. I haven't slept in two days. My body hurts. My eyes are so heavy I can barely force them open.

I can no longer remember a time when I was excited about this draft. It feels like ten years ago, but in reality it has only been a few weeks since the knights arrived in Fyrefell. I wonder where my friends ended up. I have not seen Myre or Chloe or Bogdon since arriving in the Areopagus. They were not stationed in the Areopagus's Western military sector. They could be in the East, or maybe the North, or perhaps the South. There's no telling.

But if I am struggling this hard, I can only imagine how Myre is doing. I pray silently he hasn't lost. If he is sent to the infantry, he won't receive the training he needs to survive. Inattention will cause him to die on the front lines.

I shake the worry from my head. I have protected Myre all his life, if there is any time for him to grow up and stand up for himself, it's now.

All I control is my own destiny, and although I am too tired to stand, war waits for no man or woman. I stand, collecting my helm and daggers, then follow Wisteria to the fighting fields. It is time to show these recruiters what Number 879 is capable of.

8

BELLIWHOPPING

"Drakini of Fyrefell, are you ready?" Garmin Vaid calls, completely different in appearance from when I saw him this morning. The sweat and soot is gone, showered away to reveal his glowing aureate skin.

"Ready," I reply, grabbing my daggers tight. In addition to the helm Vaid made for me, I am wearing a sleek black and gold gambeson, stuffed with armor plating. It is light and breathable, allowing me to move with little restriction. Nothing like this was offered to me my first few fights, but more weapons and equipment have become available now that five hundred draftees have been disqualified.

"Makem of Nondale, are you ready?"

My opponent smashes his sword into his shield in response, his fat tits jiggling from the impact.

"Fight!"

Makem of Nondale, you may think you are ready, but you have never seen anything like me. He has the build and demeanor of a warthog. He is short in stature and almost as wide as he is tall. His leather belt does all it can to contain the rolls of fat tucked in its embrace, the final belt hole stretching until it nearly rips completely. He wears no jerkin, probably because there is no jerkin that can fit his gelatinous upper body. Where most male warriors I've faced have muscles sculpted from marble, Makem's maker fashioned him from dough and forgot to cook him into a finished pastry.

Wherever Nondale is, it must know no famine. Makem looks like he not only has never missed a meal in his life, but that he has eaten double portions on behalf of all those who've starved. The fat in his neck gives him two additional chins brimmed with sweat, though the fight hasn't even started. He wheezes as if he's just run wind sprints before the battle began, but I was at the practice fields, and I know he was not present.

How he's made it to the final five hundred is to be determined. Fatties like this normally have unparalleled strength, so perhaps he's relied on overpowering his opponents with brute force to make it this far. He is ranked Number Seventy, so it's not like he's used to losing. But I'm not intimidated by him in the slightest. After facing Havick for what seemed like an eternity, this doughball does little to deter me.

"A woman ranked at 879 making it to day two of the tournament," Makem scoffs, his second and third chin shaking as he laughs. "This must be some cruel joke! No worries, maybe I can recruit you as a bedmaid after defeating you. You'll be put to better use there than the front lines, and you'll last longer too, if you catch my drift." He winks at me and my stomach rolls with nausea. I was going to hold back so Makem wouldn't be injured for his duties as a future infantryman, but not anymore.

Shut this fatso up with a belliwhopping, Drakini, Wisteria growls. *I would instruct you to slow time down, but I have a feeling he moves in slow motion as it is.*

I laugh inside my helm, stalking toward my opponent. He doesn't make a move toward me, to do so would likely be too much exercise for him. His cankles already strain from holding his body aloft, unnecessary movement is probably burdensome.

So many ways to attack, the opportunities are endless. He has a sword and shield, so I won't give him the pleasure of getting to cross strikes with me. If he wants to overpower me, I'll make him come to me. But do I throw my dagger at him? What are the odds of him blocking it with his shield? He is a tremendous target, it will almost feel like a wasted opportunity if I don't use it to my advantage.

I could always defeat him by exhausting him. Run laps around him until his heart explodes from exertion. But that almost feels too easy, like I wouldn't get any better out of the exchange. I need every opportunity I can seize to level up, to evolve.

But this is no opportunity—dueling this obese loser is a waste of my time. Every second I spend here is one I don't spend fighting Havick, a fighter who actually makes me better. I will make quick work of Makem, I decide.

I jog, then run, then sprint at my enemy. He roars at me as his swollen feet stagger defensively in a wide base. When we are only three strides separated, I fake a jab step right, then go left. Instinctively, he swings his sword to my right, thinking he will catch me lacking.

I carve my right dagger up the lengths of his sword arm from wrist to shoulder, then smash my left dagger's hilt in his temple. The bigger they are, the harder they fall. Makem falls hardest of them all, collapsing to the ground on top of his bleeding sword arm. I feel the ground shake around me from the impact, scoffing as I watch his back fat jiggle for several seconds.

"Do you yield?" I ask, waiting for a response. He provides none; he is unconscious from the blow to his peanut brain.

"Victor, Drakini!" Arms Master Garmin Vaid shouts, sprinting to my side to lift my hand in the air. My blood-covered dagger drips blood onto us as it's exalted above.

I eye Wisteria, who hasn't so much as moved from our starting point. She lays on the ground, licking at her paw indifferently. Her black tail flicks behind her, kicking up no dust from the ground because she isn't actually here.

She is a figment of my deteriorating mind. A product of my descent into madness. But Makem, lying at my feet? That is no hallucination. That is reality. He was ranked Number Seventy, undefeated until crossing blades from me. And now he will be sent to this undeclared war's front lines. I will advance to tomorrow, when I will be one of 250 remaining fighters.

I am Number 879, and I have prevailed once more.

Drakini, let's go, Wisteria calls, turning to leave the fields. I sheathe my daggers and follow.

"Drakini, where are you going?" Garmin calls, "Why not take a moment to savor your victory?"

"Because this is not worthy of savoring," I reply, looking at him over my shoulder. Medics rush to Makem's side and begin administering stitches to his arm-length wound. "I will be on the training yard, if you need me, readying myself for an opponent worth my time."

In the span of a few days I've evolved from one of the weakest of all draftees to a reckoning force.

9

IMAGINARY ENEMIES

I am hunted through the night by figments of my deranged imagination. I pant, too exhausted and sleep-deprived to question my lunacy. I am going on my third night of foregoing sleep in favor of training, and Wisteria has pulled out all the stops this time.

Turns out, it isn't just Havick she has the power to summon from the cracks in my mind. Tonight, I face a small battalion of foes, none of which exist outside my dark twisted fantasy.

Come back here little girl! I need to carve your flesh from your bones and make a hat and matching moccasins! Grite shouts, his manic voice spitting saliva with every word he utters.

I do the best I can to silence my breathing, any louder and they will find me. I hide hunkered down between a rack of shields and practice swords, seeking a few seconds of reprieve wherever I can.

Where weak gorl go? Havick calls out, his miniscule brain unable to piece together my disappearance.

Come out come out wherever you are;
I will find you, whether near or far;
You can run, but you can't hide;
Come out, so I can put an arrow in your side, Lu Bu says, her speech never complete without reciting rhymes.

That is how I know she is a figment of imagination; normal people do not speak in rhymes, but Lu Bu seems incapable of speaking a single sentence without following it with one that rhymes.

"There! She's behind the shields!" Osprey screeches from the air, the night's wind ruffling through her feathers. "Shit," I curse beneath my breath. The falcon-woman has the eyesight of an eagle, and she has used it to give me away every time I've found the slightest slice of rest.

Havick, Grite, Lu Bu, and Osprey. These are the opponents Wisteria summoned for me to practice against. From them, I've learned many things. Because of them, I've felt pain in ways my body never fathomed could exist. I've been beaten to a pulp over and over. These demons may be fake, but their savage blows aren't. I have lacerations on my upper arm from Osprey's talons. Bruises on my ribs from Havick's fists. A stab wound in my calf from Grite's dagger; an arrow passing through my shoulder from Lu Bu's bow.

After three days of no sleep I have no idea what's real and what's not. All I can do is trust my gut and fight based off instinct. I smile, a wave of delusion washing over me. Despite getting the shit beat out of me, I don't feel weak. Every time I've been knocked down, I've gotten back up. I am no longer the girl of Fyrefell, the girl too weak to stand up for her father, the girl so weak she allowed others to rape her.

In a matter of weeks, I've made a miraculous transformation. I've made friends with pain and embraced it as my ally. I wear it on my sleeve like a badge of honor, realizing nothing could ever hurt worse than what I've already felt. With every wound I endure I become stronger.

I grab a throwing knife from the harness I've wrapped around my leg. In it, I've sheathed over twenty throwing knives, learning I must plan for the contingency of me losing my daggers in battle. I look in the reflection of the nearest polished shield. I can see Lu Bu from here, arrow notched in her bow as she converges on my hiding spot. She may not be the closest opponent, but her arrow can reach me faster than Havick and Grite.

I stand and throw the knife directly at her, causing her to dive for cover.

Grite spots me and comes for me like a Lycan that's smelled blood. His duel wield short swords clang in the air like a challenge. I accept his challenge, retrieving two throwing knives from my thigh. I throw them sequentially in rapid fire, not to hit him, but to distract him. With his ravenous eyes tracking the blades through the air, I close the gap between us, leaping over the rack of shields.

Grite is an ugly motherfucker. His nose is fat, his eyes are too close, his teeth are crooked, and his forehead is massive. Everything that could be wrong with his face is wrong with his face. It looks like whoever bore him did so three months too early and dropped him on his underdeveloped head.

But what Grite lacks in beauty, he makes up for in fighting skills. The bastard is a devil with his blades, and I've already learned a few dozen tricks from his use of dual wielding that will carry over to my own arsenal.

Grite bats the throwing knives away with the flat of his blades and catches my first strike with his short swords, countering immediately. *There you are, my little pretty!* Slobber flies from his chapped mouth into my visor.

I can smell his rank breath through the mesh of my helm. *Time to make myself some moccasins!*

We exchange blows slow, then gradually build speed as we test each other's abilities. I don't have long, soon Lu Bu will regain footing and take aim for me, and it won't be long before Havick's brain registers I've been found.

Strike, jab, dual sidestrike, single backhand, dual downstrike. Grite laughs as he blocks my daggers like they are a child's playthings. I punch his blade away, the knuckle guard of my dagger's hilt ringing out as I avoid losing fingers by mere inches. I rain strikes down on Grite like he is the one that needs training, all while listening to him laugh like he's under a tickle attack. He screams for moccasins, says he wants my flesh so he can make a hat. I pay him no attention, forcing him to back away from my blows until he's a step away from a rack of spears. I fake a downward arc, causing him to block my blades, then plant my heel in his chest and kick off, sending him sprawling over the rack and onto his ass.

I raise my daggers just in time for Havick's four fists. Two are aimed for my head; my dagger points bury themselves into his knuckles and burrow into his wrist. He screams, but his other two fists smash into my body, sending me into the same rack of spears Grite toppled over. I land atop Grite, the laughter still escaping his body from his defeat. I wish I could find losing that hysterical, maybe then I'd be having more fun.

I steal his short swords from the ground, my daggers still buried in Havick's knuckles and forearm.

An arrow fires, gouging itself into my thigh. I let out a scream of pain, staring down at the blood that spurts from my leg. Havick uses my weakness to overwhelm me, pulverizing me into the ground until I can no longer breathe. Osprey dives, excited to catch her prey unaware. Grite picks himself up and joins in on the fun. Wisteria purrs somewhere in the distance.

When the sun rises and my delirium is over, my enemies vanish, and so too do the wounds they inflicted. My bruises are gone; my skin is cut nowhere; only my damaged ego remains.

After three days of no sleep I have no idea what's real and what's not.

My enemies may have been my imagination, as well as the wounds they inflicted on me. But the pain I felt? Whether or not it was real, I will make this pain real for someone else. In a single night, I've learned a thousand ways I can die, all so I can avoid them in reality. I praise the gods for my delusions, for they will lead to the downfall of many.

10

DO YOU YIELD?

"Tell me, do you yield?" I ask Utterson, approaching him slowly so he has time to consider the question with logic.

"To a girl? Are you mad? I'd sooner yield to a blind thief!" Utterson replies, unable to detach himself from his embarrassment. It's easy to tell when a man has never been defeated by a woman. They get all up in arms about it. Like it couldn't possibly be happening to them.

"Suit yourself."

We are in the top 250 candidates left, but I'm disappointed by my opponent's abilities yet again. Utterson is all bark and no bite. His threats fall on deaf ears when I see what he's capable of. It's like watching a kitten try to roar like a lion.

The boy's face is more acne than skin. Vicious, white-tipped pimples ready to burst open at first contact. I fear if I were to punch his cheek my gauntlet would come away with more pus than blood. He reminds me of

Grite in that way—so ugly I almost feel bad for him. But the gods didn't bless him with a kind personality to displace the ugliness, so any sympathy I feel goes down the drain. At least the uncomely boys of Fyrefell knew where they stood and had the awareness to be nice. Utterson is as scarred on the inside as he is on the outside.

He shuffles away from me on his ass, searching for the weapons he dropped somewhere in the fray of battle. I retrieve my kunai rope dart and swing the throwing knife tied to the end slowly through the air. I wasn't going to use it in this battle because I'm still learning, but after seeing the disparity between our skill levels, I could use a challenge.

The kunai rope dart was something I didn't think of until this morning, when I awoke from the delirium of last night's battles. It was the product of a hard loss and toiling over ways to get better. With Lu Bu and Osprey as new opponents, I knew I needed a way I could attack from afar and hit my enemies, while still having my daggers close at all times. If I can master the rope dart, I will master every facet of fighting.

A knife travels faster than my body. I've already perfected throwing at enemies, but attaching a rope to the equation allows my blade to move like water. Learning the rope dart is like learning to dance. It is not about thinking where the blade is, but where it will be, and anticipating its journey through the air so I can build momentum for its strike.

I am incredibly awkward with it, and Wisteria laughed at me all morning as I practiced against targets, but I'm not discouraged. It feels like such an intimate form of fighting. There is no right and wrong. There is only practice, and practice will make me perfect. Men who use bullwhips or lassos don't perfect their form in a single day, and I shouldn't be hard on myself for feeling clumsy after a few hours of practice.

I tug on the rope's knot to make sure the arrowhead-like dagger is secure, then spin it to one side, then to the other. Using the rope dart is all about feeling the blade's direction through the rope, then making it bend to your will through your body's movement. It takes me a few seconds to get adjusted to the feeling, and just as Utterson regains footing and grips his blade and shield, I am ready. I rotate my body 360 degrees and loosen my grip on the rope, letting it slip through my fingertips as my twirl fuels its trajectory. The blade obeys my body's torque and fires for Utterson, glancing off his shield and into the air.

Now is when things get tricky. I feel the blade tug me at an awkward angle as I try to adjust to its new momentum. I yank the blade back toward my body with my right hand, following through under my left armpit. The dagger follows the momentum and flies at me, still pointed away from my body. It follows my right hand and sweeps under my left armpit, the rope hugging my ribs tightly as the blade circles around my back, up my spine, and back over my right shoulder, its point aimed directly at Utterson.

I let the momentum carry out what only a flick of my wrist has started. Utterson has a dumb look on his face as he sees the blade flying at him once more. He ducks behind his shield again and deflects the strike at the last possible second.

Utterson hesitates, then charges at me. I panic, feeling awkward with the rope in my hands as the blade falls dead to the ground. I need to get around his shield if I'm to land a strike. I'm not accurate enough yet to land a hit on him with it blocking half his body. I reel the rope in, the dagger coiling across the clay ground like a snake with vertigo. Utterson commits to his charge, building speed with every stride he takes. I open my body up to him, hopefully tricking him into thinking I am ready to make a stand.

I have no idea why he thinks he can take me hand-to-hand. That is the same foolish belief that landed him on his ass last time, weapons askew on the battlefield. No matter, he will learn from this mistake a second time, and he will have time to reflect on it when he is recruited to infantry.

I spin again, this time not lifting the blade off the ground. The dagger spins with me, then fires off through the dust of the ground to wrap around Utterson's ankles. I pull the rope taut. Utterson goes to take his next step, only to find his feet can't move forward. The momentum of his body betrays him. Gravity grabs hold of him, yanking him to the ground. I hear an audible curse leave his mouth as he crashes atop his shield and his sword flies, once more, out of his hand.

I retrieve it from the dirt and hold it to the back of his neck, its point drawing blood as I press down.

"I'll ask you again, solider. Do you yield?"

I see the tension build in his body, then release all at once like a howling teapot taken off a flame. Fool him once, shame on me. Fool him twice, shame on him. He relaxes, then breathes into the dust, "I yield." The words sound like the most bitter thing he's ever tasted.

I throw his blade to the ground at his feet and unravel my rope from his ankles. "Victor, Drakini!" Garmin Vaid shouts, laughing as he sprints to join me. He lifts my arm and I take a moment to look up at the shaded recruiters, their figures too distant and shrouded by the scorching sun to be visible. They make little movement, but I can't help but wonder what they think of me now. A few days ago, they likely couldn't give two shits about me. Now, I will advance to the remaining 125 recruits of the draft for a chance at fighting the draft's fiercest competitors.

Grab your rope and meet me at the training yards. We have much to do if you plan on using that weapon on the morrow, Wisteria growls, mad that I was successful in using the rope dart against her wishes.

"Where in the world did you get the idea to use a rope dart?" Garmin asks, astounded by what he's just seen. "Never in all my years have I seen a warrior wield one of those!"

"Honestly," I answer, choosing my words before speaking recklessly. "Honestly, throwing daggers to win was just starting to feel too easy."

Garmin laughs awkwardly, uncomfortable by my answer. I step over Utterson's defeated body. Several of his pimples popped when he hit the ground face first. I do my best to not step on the pus that leaks around him.

11

THE UNDEAD

"Follow me," Garmin whispers, finger to his lips to quiet me. He's shaken me awake. It's the first time Wisteria has let me sleep in several nights, and Garmin has now ruined it. At first I think I'm hallucinating, but I have no reason to believe a dream can be this vivid. My head is a stack of disorganized papers overflowing from a rusted filing cabinet. My body is the culmination of limbs ripped apart and sewn back together improperly, or so it seems.

I move to protest but Garmin's finger firmly shushes me, then pulls my thin blanket off my half-naked body. I feel a warmth between my legs, then the cramps set in. I scramble in embarrassment, sitting up to block Garmin from seeing what's happened. I bring my hand down to my underwear and feel the blood through the darkness. I touch the sheets beneath me and feel the warm liquid seeping into my mattress. *Fuck*, I curse inwardly. Of all the nights for Garmin to wake me, of course it's this night.

I pray he can't see the mess I've made through the dimly lit barracks. My eyes squint as a cramp spasms in my uterus. I clench my teeth and breathe through the pain until it passes. "Okay, wait for me outside. I need to dress myself," I whisper, still delirious from the midnight wakeup call.

Luckily for me, he concedes to my demand and leaves as quietly as he came. I tear a piece of my pillow's silk cover and reach under my underwear, balling it up and stuffing it to soak up the never-ending flow of moon-blood. I rip the soiled underwear off and stuff it between my cot and the wall. I'll deal with it later. In less than a minute I'm fully dressed and headed out of the barracks to see what was so damn important that it couldn't wait until the morning.

"I'm sorry, but this couldn't wait," Garmin says, emerging from the shadows. "If the recruiters knew I came to tell you this, I'd be immediately terminated from my position as Arms Master, possibly worse. But—"

"Then why tell me?" I ask. "I don't want to be the reason you get in trouble, Garmin."

"I am the Arms Master, Drakini. That means I've officiated every fight of the draft and tournament so far. I know much more about your enemies than you, and I sit in on the tournament's council, along with the child King Silenius himself."

"Silenius?" I repeat the word, shocked to hear he is involved in this selection of warriors. What is a noble like him wasting time watching commoners like us beat each other to the brink of death?

"Yes, Silenius. He's been watching the fights in secret every day when time permits, and I've just come from a council meeting he called at the last minute. It's about how we are to proceed now that we've reached the top 125 candidates in all four wings of tournaments."

"We aren't proceeding the way we have been? One versus one, winner advances?"

"No, King Silenius plans on combining the remaining candidates from the North, South, East, and West military sectors. 125 draftees left in each branch, making a total of 500 survivors. He hasn't told us his exact plans yet, but he hinted at an all out free-for-all battle to see who stands victorious..."

"What do you mean 'a free-for-all'?" I ask, sleep still lifting from my brain. "This entire tournament has been a free-for-all..."

"No, this tournament has been one versus one. What Silenius has planned is a one versus 499; every man and woman for themself."

I curse inwardly, my mood souring by the second. Here I was, content on my ability to overcome enemies one at a time until I've risen to the top. Not all the training in the world can prepare me for what's coming. If Garmin's intel can be trusted, this means alliances will form amongst those at the top. Strong will hunt weak, and I have no friends to call my own in this competition.

"But there's more, Drakini, and that is the reason I woke you."

"Go on," I sigh, not sure how this could get any worse.

Garmin has a look of reluctance in his eyes. He continues, "I know you're from Fyrefell, so tell me... How much do you know about the Undead?"

I raise an eyebrow at the question. It comes out of left field with little context to support its supposition. "Very little, why do you ask?"

"Well, that's the main reason I came to you. It's time for me to give you a history lesson, because you'll be expected to fight Undead candidates."

"What do you mean!"

"Shhhhh," Garmin shushes, "Lower your voice, woman. Do you want to alert the entire barrack of our conversation?"

"What do you mean?" I repeat in a hushed tone, my voice still filled with urgency.

"I mean what I said... The Northern military sector is comprised of entirely Undead draftees. They have been holding their tournaments at night, since they cannot walk during the daylight. King Silenius has struck a peace treaty with two of the three major tribes—The Immortals and The Celestials. He's permitted them entry into the Areopagus and delegated their leaders positions of power on his council. The deal was done weeks before the draft was initiated, though word of its occurrence has been confidential until war is declared."

"What kind of war are we fighting that requires us to form an alliance with the Undead? They are bloodsuckers!" I shout with an inside voice. "They're part demon!"

"And this is exactly why I brought it to your attention now, so you have time to sit on it. Because if you go into tomorrow saying those things, their candidates will do worse than feed on you, and there is nothing I'll be able to do to stop it in the heat of competition."

"How exactly did you expect me to react? Never in all my family's years has a Sylvian King of Areopagus formed a treaty with the Undead."

"King Silenius may be a king, but he is still a teenager, Drakini. People doubt his ability to rule. There has never been a king as young as him in the history of Sylvian rulers. His parents' deaths were unexpected and untimely. Our enemies see this as an opportunity to shift the balance of power. They will do everything they can to usurp the throne, so Silenius did the only thing he saw possible. He signed a deal with the devil. But that's enough on politics, the public policy reasons behind this decision are far above my pay grade. I am here to make sure you survive, and to do that, I need you to go into this with an open mind."

"So what, I'm expected to defeat the same species that feeds on us for food just to win this stupid tournament?"

"You're expected to win, Drakini. That's what all of this is about. You're human. King Silenius wants to see if humans can keep up with the Undead. After watching days of candidates, I know in my heart you are the only one who can. The Undead... They may be cursed, but I've traveled the past few nights to the Northern sector and watched them fight. They are stronger than us humans. They are faster. More savage. Less inclined to show mercy. And to put the cherry on top, they fly."

"It just doesn't make any sense... The Undead hate us. Father used to say they think we are an inferior species. Said in some regions of the world they enslave us as bloodbags and sustain our lives only to feed off us. Collect humans like cattle and impregnate women like livestock farmers."

"Times are changing, and we too must change with them," Garmin explains, his fearful face doing little to reassure me. "I'm going to tell you everything I know about them, but first, you must follow me."

"Where... Where are we going?" I stutter.

"To the Northern military sector. Tonight is their final tournament to select their final 125 candidates. I want you to see what these demons are capable of."

12

BLOODSUCKERS

The Areopagus is vast, and the hike to the Northern military sector was long. Blood seeps from my shedding uterus and fights the silk I've stuffed in its place. I do my best to distract myself with conversation, but the cramps nag at the back of my mind. Wisteria prowls in the distance, scouting ahead and falling behind, always sticking to the shadows even though the sane-minded can't see her. I can see her yellow eyes from the shadows, and she stalks in silence as she stews over the things Garmin has told me.

I've gathered much from Garmin in our trek. I realize how little I know about the Undead as he dispels rumors and brings new information to light. In Fyrefell, we had no Lycans or Undead living in our midst. Monsters such as those were shunned from entry into the city, and our close-knit community was ever-weary of strangers.

Garmin has taught me of the Undead's origin. Father told me bits and pieces as a child, but never to this extent, and never with this much clarification. At the beginning, there was the Creator, and he created all we know and love on this precious earth. To protect his Creation, he made the sun, Solis, and the moon, Luna. Solis was the protector of the day, and it was Luna's duty to guard us in the night.

But the god of the day and the goddess of night lusted over one another from across the horizon, drawn to each other's embrace. Eventually, after hundreds of years in orbit, they eclipsed, and from Luna's body twin sons were born, named Dagon and Damon.

Infatuated with each other's love, Solis and Luna remained eclipsed and delegated their duty of protecting creation to their sons. Dagon was selected to protect the world in the night in Luna's absence, and Damon was chosen to guard humanity during the daytime. But when the Creator learned of the sun and moon's treachery, he brought forth curses on Dagon and Damon to punish them for their parents' sins. Because of the Creator's curse, Damon was made so he could never walk in the daylight again, and Dagon was forced to turn into a foul beast in the night.

Together, Dagon and Damon wreaked havoc on earth, multiplying their offspring and spreading their curses across the globe. Damon's offspring became known as the Undead, children of the night who feed off the blood of mortals in order to satisfy their bloodlust. Dagon's descendants became known as Lycans, wolfmen unable to control the beasts within them whenever the moon is full.

I knew these fables in bits and pieces before my talk with Garmin, but I knew nothing of the ancient Undead Tribes.

The Celestials, an ancient tribe of Undead that immigrated to this kingdom thousands of years ago from Bloodhaven. Known for their iconic silver hair and lilac hue eyes, they are the oldest and proudest tribe of

Undead in existence. They claim themselves to be the purest of stock the Undead have to offer, declaring it punishable by death to produce offspring outside the Celestial bloodline.

The Immortals, a tribe native to the Western coast's Thoren Mountains. Their hair, like Celestials, is a mixture of silver and gray, and it's said their origin was created by a renegade group of Undead rebelling against the Celestials and seceding from their faction centuries ago. The rebellion became known as Crankshaw's Rebellion, named for the founder of the Immortals and the man who raised arms against the Celestials. To date, the civil war between Celestials and Immortals is the bloodiest occurrence in all of history. Millions died, and many more were injured. To this day, there is an underlying animosity between the tribes' descendants that time has failed to heal.

Lastly, there is the Godhand, who are not a part of Silenius's treaty. Unlike the Celestials and Immortals, you are not born into the Godhand, rite of entry is earned through blood. The Godhand are an outcast faction of Undead—those not born into pureblood families who perceive themselves as superior. Their physical characteristics are different. When an Undead's blood becomes muddled with mortals, some lose their purple eyes to a perverse shade of red. Most Godhand, it is said, have midnight black hair and eyes red as rubies. No one outside their faction knows the price they must pay for entry, but members of the Godhand bear its mark—they each have holes gouged through their palms from wooden stakes, their bodies unable to heal wounds incurred by such a weapon. Regardless of appearance, that is the identifier of a Godhand, for they have faced that which can kill them, and they have risen above its infirmities.

There are hundreds of other castes too, but these are the most ancient and sacred lines of Undead. Many families have left their control and went off to start lives in the outskirts of the kingdom's region. From them, the

Undead curse has spread without census, burrowing into the hillsides and under mountains far from the king's power to control.

The Undead are separated by their infallible prides yet united in their hatred of Lycans and humanity. For eons, their diet has consisted of fresh blood preyed upon through force. They are humanity's greatest predator, but their hunt does not kill its victim. It's a paradox, because they think themselves superior to humans yet rely on them entirely for food. Although they can feed on the blood of animals, very few do, and so they would seemingly cease to exist without humanity's survival.

"Here," Garmin whispers, stopping me in my tracks. "Here is a good vantage point for us to watch." I squat next to him, then lay flat on my belly to avoid being seen. We lay on a crested hill that has a perfect aerial view of the fighting fields below. On the opposite side of us, far across the fields of drilling Undead, sits the recruiters, their identities masked by the darkness of night.

Their Arms Master, unlike Garmin Vaid, is Undead like the rest of them. Their fighting fields are different from ours in the Western sector. There, we have nothing more than a clay pit surrounded by a stadium. Here though, it looks like the Areopagus's funds have spared no expense erecting this state-of-the-art facility. The ground is granite, the weapons are new, the stadium is polished titanium, and the instructors are adept with decades of experience. Comparing it to the Western sector, this place looks like a crisp lake whereas ours looks like an ancient latrine.

"In the far corner, ranked Number One of 1,000, is Ventur of Tribe Celestial!" the Arms Master calls. I eye the fighter. He is like something from a story book, the sort of warrior I didn't know could exist in reality. He has closely cut silver hair with purple eyes bright enough to be seen from a hundred yards away. His armor is lean like his body. The look in his eyes resembles that of a tiger. His chiseled jawline is sharp enough to cut papyrus. He holds his sword like a man born with it in his cradle.

Wisteria disappears from my side and walks down the hill, likely going to get a closer look at the fighters. I don't call after her, not wanting to give myself and Garmin away, but also not wanting Garmin to think I'm a lunatic for talking to something that isn't really there.

"Standing opposed in the near corner is Monolith of Tribe Immortal!" This fighter lives up to his name. He is like a giant of unbelievable proportion. He is built like a brick shithouse. Standing head and shoulders taller than Ventur, who is tall himself, this man is twice the width of the Celestial Undead. Like Makem of Nondale, Monolith fights shirtless, but unlike Makem of Nondale, there isn't an ounce of fat to be seen on his body. Muscles protrude from his thick neck to his tapered waist, reminding me of Havick's build. He is a genetic freak, his hands big enough to likely squeeze my head like an orange until not a drop of pulp is left. Long, gray hair is pulled back in a ponytail. In Monolith's right hand is a trident with three sharpened prongs. In his left is a cat o' nine tails, a whip with nine lashes that each have barbed endings.

Neither fighter wears a helm to protect their head. For some, the risk is worth the reward, enabling a warrior to fight with their vision unobscured. Unlike me, men like this have not had their brains bashed to the point of seeing hallucinations. I envy them for this in some respects, but without Wisteria, I would not be the fighter I am.

"Fight!" the Undead Arms Master shouts. Instantly, Ventur levitates from the ground, taking flight over his opponent. Monolith remains grounded, coiling his whip on the ground like a snake preparing to strike. The whip looks to have a reach of fifteen feet from my viewpoint. Ventur hovers over his opponent at twice that length, sizing Monolith up from afar before engaging.

I spot Wisteria as she hops over the fighting field's fence and sits in the corner of the arena, tail swiping the granite behind her as she eagerly awaits the inevitable. She will watch these fighters with objective curiosity and tailor my training to prepare me for their opposition. I cringe at the thought of what's to come.

"It's a fight, not a staring contest," Monolith shouts up at his opponent. "Are you going to come down here or what?"

"I quite enjoy seeing you look as small as an ant from up here, thank you very much," Ventur replies, calm and composed. There is an undeniably handsome quality in Ventur's confident smirk. It is almost enough to make me smile, though I don't know what I'm giddy about.

Monolith cracks his whip against the empty air below Ventur. Ventur mocks him by pretending to be scared. Ventur readjusts his body and dives like a predatory bird. Monolith rears back his whip and lashes a second time, this time going for the killshot. The barbed ends coil for Ventur's body but ricochet off Ventur's shield as he bats them away. Ventur rotates his body in the air like a twirling arrow, then shoves the narrow side of his shield into Monolith's clavicle. The shield's momentum from Ventur's rotating makes it a deadly strike. I hear the collarbone snap from here and echo across the arena.

Monolith grunts as he fights to stay afoot. His trident is too long and awkward to hit Ventur in close quarters. Instead, Monolith takes his whip and wraps it around Ventur's neck, choking him. The desperate attack is quickly overcome as Ventur slips his blade between himself and Monolith, cutting the leather whip from Monolith's handle. The tension around his neck disappears and the leathery cord drops to the ground.

Monolith chokes up on his trident and strikes for Ventur's midsection. It clangs off the Undead's shield. Ventur ducks down and jumps up, the upperside of his shield striking the underside of Monolith's chin, breaking his jaw with the strike. Ventur takes the broadside of his shield and smashes it into his opponent's nose, cracking Monolith's face and drawing blood from his nostrils. This Undead is deadly, I realize. He hasn't even swung his sword and is well on his way to felling an opponent twice his size and strength.

He's fast. So fast I can barely register his change of direction. It's like watching a hare box a tortoise. Monolith rears back his trident but is stopped as Ventur slits his wrist. The severed ligaments cause Monolith to drop his weapon completely. The giant is defenseless to protect himself as Ventur whips his shield around into Monolith's cheekbone, followed by a quick hamerstrike on Monolith's opposite clavicle. Ventur kicks in the Undead's knee, snapping the ligaments that hold it in place and causing it to buckle backward. The giant falls with a mighty thud. Ventur raises his shield above his head and puts all his weight into a final strike. He slams down the narrow side of the shield into Monolith's sternum. We all hear the audible crack it makes. Wisteria's tail is no longer wagging behind her. She sees the savagery this species brings to their fighting style. It is leagues beyond what humans are capable of.

The Arms Master calls the fight, and Ventur licks his opponent's blood from the splatter that drips down his face.

"Ventur of Tribe Celestial, victor!" Ventur smirks coyly as his arm is raised above his body. It doesn't seem he's so much as broken a sweat from the altercation. Not a single hair is out of place. His breathing isn't labored. He is a conditioned fighting machine. It's evident these demons have been fighting since birth. Their sense of entitlement over humanity makes sense, if this is what they're capable of.

I try to still my beating heart but can't. I can't tell if I'm nervous or excited or afraid. No one has ever made me feel this small and powerless without directly hurting me. It makes me want to wipe that arrogant smile off Ventur's face. I'm mad at him, and I don't even know the slightest thing about him. But I know enough. He's a damn bloodsucker. Without humans he would be nothing. He relies on our veins to reap his glory.

"This isn't over!" Monolith screams, blood flying from between his missing teeth. While I've been daydreaming, I completely missed the fact that Monolith has risen from defeat and snuck behind Ventur. I gasp as the giant Undead throws himself at Ventur while he stands with his arm raised and back turned. It happens so fast I nearly miss it. With the speed of a god, Ventur shoves the Arms Master out of the way and ducks down, not even able to see Monolith's body as it sails over his back. One moment Ventur is there, Monolith ready to break him with a single strike, and the next, Monolith is grasping thin air. It's like the victor has eyes in the back of his head and saw the attack coming from a mile away.

Monolith crashes to the ground in defeat a second time, instantly squirming to get back to his feet. Ventur doesn't give him that chance. "Easy big fella," Ventur laughs, sword drawn with its tip touching the back of Monolith's neck. "One move and I'll sever your spinal cord. It will bring me no pleasure to see you dragged out of here on a stretcher. Do us both a favor and yield. I have already been declared victor."

Monolith lays on his stomach with his arms ready to push himself back up. He remains still, weighing his options for a few seconds. I realize I'm holding my breath and biting my tongue.

After what feels like an eternity, Monolith replies, his voice somber and placid, "We Immortals do not yield to Celestials."

Ventur's grin fades at the declaration. "Then you, Immortal, will die at the hands of a Celestial."

I gasp as Ventur's sword inserts itself into Monolith's neck at an upward angle, driving itself into his skull until the giant's brain is severed in two. Monolith's blood pools along the granite. There is no reaction from the recruiters other than a brief moment of them scribbling on their notepads. The Arms Master dusts himself off. Ventur pushed him so hard he slid several feet across the granite ground.

"So they don't only hate humans," I whisper to Garmin Vaid, who lays beside me equally filled with shock. "They hate each other too."

That is how we humans can win the battle to come. Not by overcoming their powers, but by sowing discord against these demons. I see now how deep the rivalry goes between Tribe Celestial and Tribe Immortal. They would rather die than be defeated; their prides cannot handle surrender.

I smile as clouds blot out the moon above. Wisteria looks over her shoulder at me, thinking the same thing I am no doubt. There is no need to defeat them if they will willingly go to war against each other.

13

VENTUR OF TRIBE CELESTIAL

"I n the far corner is Nikolai of Tribe Celestial!" Arms Master shouts as the next fight approaches. It took a while for the medics to remove Monolith's corpse from the granite pit. His massive body required five humans to lift him, and no Undead offered to provide their supernatural strength to aid in speeding the process. The night is only so long, so as soon as his body was removed, the next two fighters entered the fighting field, each of them eyeing the puddle of blood from Monolith's downfall.

Nikolai is similar to Ventur in height and build but has no shield or sword. Instead, he fights with a weapon I've never seen before. From each hip, he draws a metal pole with a sharpened tip, each the length of his arm. He warms his muscles by swinging them, then striking the air in front of him a few times. Then, when he is satisfied, he brings their butt ends together and twists in a screwing motion. The baton-length shafts snap together into a dual-edged spear the length of a staff.

Because its length is made from steel, its body can be used to deflect a sword and its ends can be used for striking. It is a multi-purpose weapon. Nikolai can throw it like a spear, break it in two like dual swords, and strike his opponent with a staff. It's ingenious, now that I think about it.

"I've never even thought of making something like that in the Forge," Garmin whispers. "The Undead are dozens of years ahead of us in their weapon design it seems."

I grunt in acknowledgement, then focus my eyes on Nikolai's opponent.

"In the near corner is Anabelle of Tribe Celestial!" Arms Master yells. The woman before us is gorgeous as the Northern Star. She is lean and toned like a sprinter. Her armor is skintight and adheres to her body like a glove, exposing her curves for my eyes to envy. She is built like me with the addition of a thicker ass and bigger boobs. Her long, silver hair is pulled back in a bun for battle, but it sparkles nonetheless under the moon's glow.

This is the sort of woman that men want to be with and women want to be. Her skin is pale from lack of daylight exposure, but she somehow makes her paleness attractive. She licks her blood red lips as she readies her sword. Instead of a conventional shield, her nondominant arm wears a gauntlet with boosted protection. Built into her forearm's armor is her shield so she doesn't have to carry it. The shield is flared and wide at her elbow but tapers down to a single point where her fingers end. It is an elegant design, lightweight enough to wield easily yet durable enough to defend against blows.

"Fight!" Both warriors take to the sky and charge each other. It's easy to track their movement in the darkness because their pale faces contrast the black backdrop. They exchange no pleasantries like Ventur and Monolith before. These are both Celestials, Undead cut from the same cloth with no animosity held toward the other for the status of their birth. This fight is not about status, it is about duty. They both know what is at stake and have been preparing for this showdown their whole life it seems.

Nikolai breaks his spear in two and holds one like a sword, extending out from his body, and the other like a dagger, its point facing back toward his elbow.

Anabelle attacks first, swinging her sword in a downward arc intent on cutting Nikolai in two at his shoulder. Nikolai drops through the air several feet, avoiding the blow altogether, then ducks under Anabelle's feet, rising behind her, jabbing his sword-positioned spear for her back. She spins and deflects the strike with her shielded forearm, grunting as she does so.

I can see the ferocity on her face now that she faces my direction. This is the kind of woman I want to be. She's a force worth fearing. Her purple eyes burn like gemstones on fire. But Nikolai is calm and composed. He parries her next strike and rains his twin spears down on her like they are dancers in the ballet. The fighters ebb and flow through the open air as they strike, deflect, spin, and strike again. It's like watching a well-choreographed dance more than a brawl for a victor. It's beautiful. It's violent. It's everything the Western military sector's fights are missing. Us humans are not trained to battle like this. We fight hard, but there is no method to our madness. We fight for survival. These two fight as if fighting is an art.

I'm so drawn in toward the action that I don't hear an intruder approach from behind. I have no idea how long Garmin and I are watched by our newly arrived guest. I hear no footfall. All I hear is someone's nostrils sniffing the air, followed by the calm clearing of a throat.

"Now now, what do we have here?" His voice is calm and sultry. I jerk around, reaching for my waist instinctively but realize I have no weapons on me. As I spin to face our guest, my neck is met with the tip of a sword blade. "Ah ah ah, let's not do anything stupid."

The first thing I remember seeing are his eyes. His deep, velvety, lilac eyes. They glow through the night like purple lightning. In his eyes a storm rages. A mix of lavender and violet and amethyst clouds seeking to devour the sky, each color rolling over the other. They're tantalizing, easy for me to get lost in. And then I see his face, instantly recognizable from the fight we just witnessed.

"Ventur," I say with a forced smile, trying to conceal my fear. Looming over us is the same Undead who just bested a behemoth of a demon, his sword tip dried with the blood of Monolith's dead body. Garmin makes no sudden movement beside me. He, too, lays on his back and stares up at our captor.

"We were just—" Garmin starts. Ventur interrupts him, "Don't get so tight, human. Do I look stupid? I know exactly what you were doing. You came to get a little sneak peak at Undead excellence. Can't say I blame you. I'm sure you're half bored out of your minds fighting other humans down in the..." He sniffs the air around us, locking in our scent. "Southern military sector?" He sniffs the air one more time. "Wait, no... Forgive me! Western military sector! I'm sure of it. You both smell of rusted weapons and overflowing latrines."

I scowl at his comment, but I'm not surprised at his arrogance. If I had even a fraction of his fighting skills, I'd probably be an egomaniac too. "Anyway, don't worry. I'm no snitch," he smiles through the dark. "However, the only reason I found you both was because I smelled..." He licks his lips, silently pausing to look directly at me. "Blood. I smelled blood." Ventur moves his eyes from my face to my thighs, his fangs exposed through his smile.

Fuck, I curse, my heart panicking. I nearly forgot from all the excitement that my moonblood is leaking! I've compromised us. If Ventur was able to smell me bleeding from hundreds of yards away, there's no telling what other Undead have picked up on our scent.

I turn to face Garmin, then whisper, "The moon has made me bleed..." A look of horror possesses my Arms Master's face. I continue, "I had no idea they could..."

"You're human," Ventur interjects. "I surmise there's much you are ignorant about. Now, I hate to do this, but you have two options here. During my fight, I worked up quite the appetite. The blood rations your child king supplies us Undead is quite stale. I'd prefer celebrating with a bit of... fresh blood... And after smelling your moonblood floating, I simply can't help myself. Now, the way I see it, you can both pay my small fee and I will send you on your way before others pick up on your smell... Or... I can turn you both in for spying on foreign military sectors without the council's leave. Which will it be?"

I look to Garmin, hoping he has something that can get us out of this. I am panicking again. Memories of my head being held to the ground while knights take me from behind set in. I feel powerless. I've just seen what this warrior is capable of. Asking for permission to feast on our blood was a mere formality. This demon could hold us in the dirt and take what he wants from us if he so pleased. I hate his cocky smile. I hate his handsome face. I hate his beautiful eyes. The gods have given this man everything and loosed him on the world to take even more.

I hear a growl from behind him and see Wisteria's golden eyes glowing through Ventur's spread legs. She looks at me with contempt, knowing I am moments away from submitting to this demon's internal desires. As I stare into her venomous eyes, I am reminded I am more than my past weaknesses. I am not the fragile girl who was broken by the world. I was Number 879, one of the weakest of humanity's recruits, yet I've advanced to the top 125. Ventur may have years of training and experience on me, but he has one thing in common with my enemies. He underestimates me.

"I have a third option," I whisper, cringing as his blade presses deeper into my neck.

"Oh, do you now?" he chuckles. "You're lucky I'm in a good mood after my win, so I will hear you out, human."

"Fight me for our blood," I reply, afraid to look away from Wisteria for fear of giving into my cowardice. She nods at me approvingly for making my proposal. "If I win, you let us go. If you win, we will both give you the blood you seek and be on our merry way."

"Ha!" Ventur mocks my offer, a crazed look on his face. The adrenaline of his fight with Monolith remains. "What makes you think I'm inclined to waste my time sparring with a piece of meat like you? I'm the one with everything to gain and you're the one with everything to lose."

"If you have nothing to lose then it should be no problem dealing with a weakling like me," I smirk, insulting his pride. I've watched Ventur fight, and I know his ego is the most fragile part of his identity. I know it before he answers, this man can't back down from what I've just challenged him to. Anything less would be an insult to his superiority complex.

"Fine," he sighs, removing the blade from my neck with reluctance. "But I warn you, I won't go easy just because you are a girl."

"I wouldn't expect anything less," I reply, standing to look him in the eyes.

"Victor, Nikolai of Tribe Celestial!" the Undead Arms Master shouts from behind me.

"Fuck," Ventur curses under his breath. "I had fifty coppers on Anabelle. Damn Nikolai; that runt never knows when to quit." Ventur spits on the ground and focuses back on me. "Follow me, we don't have all night."

14

MOUSE VERSUS LION

"Are you fucking crazy?" Garmin asks as he helps me slip into a jerkin. Ventur has led us to the Northern military sector's practice yards. Here, like the fighting fields, the facilities are also vastly superior to the Western precinct's practice area. In fact, these practice fields are nicer than our actual arena, which is a slap in the face to admit.

Regardless, Wisteria has stilled my nerves. Ventur may be Undead, but he puts his boots and gauntlets on like any regular human. My uterus spasms as I fasten the jerkin and examine the racks of weapons for something suitable for my fighting style.

"I didn't exactly see you jumping up and down with a solution," I reply. I have bled through the pillow linens stuffed in my privates and now stain my pants enough for Garmin to see. "Besides, it's my fault we were caught. I didn't know their kind could smell my moonblood from so far away."

"I'm an idiot for bringing us here," Garmin concludes, panicking. "I've put my job at stake. Creator's sake, I've put our lives at stake." He runs his hand through his thick black hair nervously.

"Would you relax? Geez, you're making me nervous." He is like a tea pot boiling over, his anxiety spewing out of his mouth and onto his feet, splashing me in its collateral damage.

"How could you not be nervous? Huh? We just watched this blood-sucker kill a bloodsucker twice his size!"

"He offered him the chance to yield first," I defend, the reality of my decision setting in. "Now a little less talking and a little more helping me figure out what weapon I can use to beat him."

Garmin sighs and resorts back to what he knows best—being an Arms Master. He examines the racks of weapons with scrutiny, walking between them while Ventur waits for us on the opposite side of the field.

"Stalling won't work," Ventur calls. "Daylight is still three hours away!"

"He fights with sword and shield," Garmin whispers to himself, analyzing my options, "And he can fly. You won't win in a battle of hand to hand with him. Not even Monolith could do that. So your best bet is to keep your distance and rely on your throwing abilities. At least that's something that goes in your favor. But if you throw a dagger and miss, you're in for a world of pain. That leaves us with only one option..." Garmin grabs a spear and breaks its shaft at the spearhead's base. He then grabs a chain that's tied around the rack's base to keep it from being moved. He breaks the chain with a hammer from one of the racks and weaves its links through a hole on the spearhead's butt end.

In a matter of seconds, Garmin has made a rope dart for me to wield against my Undead opponent, something that brings me little joy to see. I have only practiced with the rope dart for a single day, and my fight against Utterson is proof I'm less than proficient with its fighting style. But still,

Garmin is right. Ventur can fly, and I'll need to keep him at a distance if I'm to win. I can't risk throwing daggers at him for fear of him dodging my attack. I need something I can throw and easily retrieve. The rope dart is the only chance I have at beating this Undead, and the chance itself is rather slim.

I spin the makeshift weapon in my hand, not used to having a chain in place of a rope. It's slightly heavier, but that will make the spearhead's momentum faster and stronger. I close my eyes and get a feel for its weight. I tie the chain in a slip knot around my anchor hand and warm my muscles. I spin it by my side, then over my head like a lasso, then windmill it around the inside of my bicep, twisting my torso so my arm releases its spin on the opposite side of my body. I let it wrap around the outside of my same arm and pull its rotation back to my strong side.

I let the momentum die and nod to Garmin that I'm ready. I realize he's mesmerized by what I've just done. The chain moves so fast it's hard for spectators to track its movement, making my wielding look like some form of sorcery. But there is no magic in what I do, it is just perpetual movement and momentum. With a weapon like this, you can't stop moving. It's like dancing, always planning your next steps seconds in advance, hoping your choreography doesn't fail you.

I leave Garmin behind to claim my spot on the practice field, eyeing Ventur from several dozen yards away. His pale face shines through the night, his lilac eyes staring at me with adoration. Does he think I'm cute, like some mouse standing up to a lion? Or does he respect my bravery? Probably the former, but I will teach him respect as our fight progresses.

"Shall we?" Ventur asks, his feet leaving the ground as he takes to the sky. My heart is hammering in my chest. I know how important the first seconds of this fight are. This is when he will underestimate me the most, which gives me the advantage. The longer I last, the harder he will try, and the harder it will be for me to defeat him. I need to come out with a bang and catch him lacking. That is the only way I'll win this duel.

He dives with his sword cocked and shield protecting center body mass. I spin my chain to build up speed, then shoot it in his direction. It isn't long enough to reach him, but him seeing the spear point makes him falter slightly to the side. I pull back with my anchor hand and let the chain's rotational plane wrap around my knee, allowing it to redirect aimed at him again. It lashes out, chains rattling, this time striking his shield.

I don't give him time to think as I pull back with my anchor and let the chain wrap around my foot, kicking out to the side and back at him again. Ventur strikes the spearhead with his sword, throwing the chain's momentum in a different course. I feel its direction through my body and ride with it, spinning my body with torque so the chain rotates around me and fires again at him. Ventur's brows furrow with shock as the spearhead he just knocked away is already on target to hit him again. In less than ten seconds I've managed to nearly hit him four times.

He drops in altitude to avoid the swinging strike and moves to close the gap between us. I pull with my anchor hand and windmill around my strong side, then opposite side, then back to my strong side, releasing the spearhead in his direction a fifth time. He swings his sword to smack the chain away, but his strike has unintended consequences. Instead of blocking the strike, my chain wraps around his sword and I pull with my anchor hand, wrenching it from his grasp and flinging it to the ground.

I shake my chain free of the sword and pull it back to my body. I pull under my strong arm and over my weak shoulder, firing another shot immediately. Ventur bats the strike away with his shield and closes the gap further, now only a few short feet from me. He's smiling as I yank the chain back and prepare for my next strike.

Ventur sees his gap and takes it, raising his shield with his arm and preparing to bring it down on me like he did when he broke Monolith's clavicle. His body flies through the air faster than a tyrfalcon. His strike will be powerful enough to do more than break bone; it will shatter my body from neck to toe. I shoot my spearhead in his direction and dive beneath him. The chain wraps around his neck and the tension follows my body as I slide under him, flipping him midair and pulling him to the earth. Ventur crashes to the ground face first as I stand behind him, yanking my chain free of his neck and back into orbit around my body.

Now it is me who smiles. I fire my next shot as he gets his feet under him and he barely avoids the strike by a fraction of a second. His fangs bit into his bottom lip when he landed, forcing him to bleed. He raises his free hand and touches his bloodied lip, then licks it with his tongue.

"Bloodbag whore," he snaps, throwing his shield at me. I've provoked the monster inside him. I dive to the ground to avoid the flying shield, standing just in time to be tackled by Ventur's shoulder. The wind leaves my lungs as we crash to the ground. My vision goes blurry as a rain of fists shower into me. My body goes number with each blow I take. My skin splits open above my cheekbone from one of his punches. My nose throbs as he fractures it with another. I'm doing everything I can to defend myself, raising my forearms to catch the majority of the blows.

"I'll show you, deplorable human," he growls as he falls into a rhythm. Through the mirage of pain, I'm able to find the spearhead lying on the ground next to me. I grab it with my hand and raise it perpendicular to his strikes. In Ventur's rage, he's unable to process I now have a weapon raised against him, and his fist punches directly into its point, severing his knuckles and fist in half.

I hear a grunt of pain, then a moan of agony as the spear cuts his hand down the middle. I can barely see what's happening through my swollen eyes.

Now! I hear Wisteria growl from a world away. *He's hurt! Submit him now!*

Somehow, through nothing more than instinctual fury, I grab hold of the loose chain lying around me. I wrap it around his neck and pull with all my might. Ventur screams in frustration, then gurgles. He stands to his feet, pulling at the lasso that cuts off his blood supply. Then, like a panicking animal, he makes a fatal mistake. Ventur takes flight like a child trying to run from its fears. I hold tight to the chain as I'm ripped from the ground, suspended in flight as Ventur's bleeding fist spits blood on my face. He takes off into the night to shake the grip I have over him, but I won't let go.

My entire body's weight is now dangling from his neck, cutting the oxygen from his brain. He tries to break free by snapping the coil, but his severed hand is too weak and slick with blood to get a proper grasp. I see veins bulging from his pale forehead as we levitate ten, twenty, now thirty feet above the ground. Quickly, his flight loses steam as his mind loses consciousness.

I cry with hysteria, "You want blood so bad, suck on your own you fucking demon spawn!"

We are losing altitude now as he loses to my chokehold. Tears are welling in my eyes as we plummet to the earth below. I don't remember hitting the ground. I just remember smiling wide as everything goes black.

15

NOBODY WANTS TO BE A NOBODY

I wake with the reassurance of bruises and lacerations to prove to myself last night was not a nightmare or hallucination. I am back in my cot in the barracks. My body feels like it was dropped from the sky. Well, that's because it technically was, my memory reminds me. I was dangling in the open air, my homemade chain rope dart wrapped around Ventur's neck, then all of a sudden we were both plummeting.

My pillow case is still torn, my sheets are still bloody, and I am still dressed from last night's battle. My head aches, a sharp pain setting in behind my eyes. It feels like they're being melted from the inside. Fever riddles my body from exhaustion. But none of these pains are enough to wipe the smile off my face. I did it. I beat an Undead in battle. Though I won by hairline margins, I won nonetheless. And not to just any Undead. Ventur of Tribe Celestial, the cream of the crop.

It doesn't feel real. It feels like any moment I'm going to wake up and learn this is all some dream. That I'll wake up and still be the fragile girl from the irrelevant, backwater town called Fyrefell. That instead of competing in the top 125, I'll instead be playing stickball for bragging rights with kids who will grow up to be nobodies in this world.

I left Fyrefell because I don't want to be a nobody. I want to make a name for myself. A beacon of hope to commoners all around that they can make more of their lives. That they don't have to struggle to put food and water on the table every night; that they don't have to fear losing their mothers to bandits or their daughters to lusty knights.

I swing my legs to the side of my bed and nearly step on Wisteria's sleeping body. I can feel her purr vibrating the floor around her. For the first time since her inception, she is calm and undemanding. She never lets me sleep in like this. Perhaps she is proud of my victory last night. Or perhaps she herself is finally tired from all the all-nighters we've spent training.

Our barracks are nearly empty. Though there are 125 of us remaining, this housing unit is large and long, and there are many more empty beds than occupied ones. I lean over and look down the row of cots. It seems I'm the only body that remains. The rest of our group must be out training or eating, probably the latter since I rarely see other draftees on the practice fields.

Today is the day. Today we will go to war against the remaining draftees, with only one victor permitted to reign supreme. Thanks to Garmin, I now know what I'm up against. Thanks to Garmin, I have the upper—

"Shit," I curse under my breath, "Garmin!"

I nearly trip over Wisteria as I throw myself from bed in a panic. I was so caught up reveling in last night's win that I didn't even think about Garmin. Is he okay?

Did Ventur snitch on us?

Has he lost his job?

Or has something worse happened?

The possibilities are endless, and my pretend scenarios get worse with each passing second. I need to get to the Forge. Need to make sure Garmin is safe. It was my moon bleeding that got us caught, and I won't be able to live with myself if I'm the reason Garmin now faces consequences for us both. I nearly break the barrack's door off its hinges with how fast I sprint to the Forge.

Reality blurs as I hold back tears. I don't know why I'm crying. Well, yes I do. I am always over-emotional when the moon makes me bleed. But still, the thought of losing Garmin Vaid is something worth crying over. He has been there for me in ways no one else has. He has shown me kindness when I didn't deserve it. I need to make this right.

The sweltering heat of the Forge attacks me as I nearly slip on the thick coat of ash that covers the floor. "Garmin Vaid! I need to speak to Garmin Vaid!" I shout at the nearest blacksmith as he looks up from the sword he smelts like I'm a deranged lunatic.

"Not here," he grunts, wiping sweat and soot from his brow. "Was called to the recruiters council for Arms Master business. Wouldn't tell us what for."

Fuck! I scream, turning to sprint, then nearly fall on my ass as Garmin looks in from outside the Forge.

"Ah look at that. You found him!" the blacksmith laughs sarcastically. "Speak his name and he shall appear. Now I can get back to my work." The blacksmith returns to smelting iron, unbothered by my manic energy.

"Garmin," I gasp, "I thought... I thought you..."

"Shhhh," he whispers, "Not here. Let's go for a walk."

I follow him outside and join his side, nearly bursting at the seams for details on what happened last night. Garmin begins the conversation before I can ask questions, "How are you feeling?"

"I'm fine," I grunt, then add, "I was worried sick about you."

"You, worried about me?" Garmin laughs. "I'm not the one that got beat half to death by an Undead last night."

"First off, I won that fight," I defend, punching his arm playfully but hard enough to make sure it hurts a little. "And second, what the hell happened? Are we in trouble for being caught by Ventur?"

"If you think that arrogant brat is going to go tell his superiors he got beat by a human last night, you're dumber than I thought. Ventur will keep his mouth shut. If he doesn't, he'll damn near be excommunicated from Tribe Celestial. And as for what happened, I had to carry your unconscious body after you and him crash landed on granite ground. You're lucky you didn't break a leg in the fall or crack your head open."

"Well what about Ventur? Did he let you leave without demanding blood?"

"He passed out midair. He was knocked unconscious when he hit the ground, and for obvious reasons, I didn't stick around and wait for him to wake up. Drakini," Garmin Vaid pauses, grabbing my arm and staring down at my eyes. "We got incredibly lucky last night. We could be hanged for spying. Or worse, we could be sent to the infantry's front lines. We are in the clear for now, but you can't tell anyone what happened. I know you're proud of yourself for belliwhopping an Undead. I'm proud of you too. But no one can know."

"I have no one to tell," I smile back at him. "After all, you're the only friend I have."

16

DEN OF VIPERS

I am panting so hard that I fear the atmosphere doesn't have enough oxygen to satisfy my lungs. Sweat sinks its stingers into my eyes. Hunger gnaws at me, making me nauseous. My abdomen spasms with cramps. My head aches from last night's pummeling. The sun scorches my exposed flesh more with every passing second.

I have never been so close to death, yet I have never felt so alive.

You're the one that wanted to use that stupid rope as a weapon, Wisteria purrs. *Now prove to me it's more than luck that won last night.*

I whip my rope back to me with my anchor hand and send it flying for Grite. My opponent chuckles, crossing his swords over his sternum to protect his center mass. Good thing I wasn't aiming for center mass. The spearhead at the end of the rope bites into his bicep, causing him to laugh outrageously at the pain. Grite is a masochist through and through, and I've never known him to find anything but pleasure in being wounded.

With my rope dart anchored in Grite's bicep on one end and my hand on the other, I flick the midpoint of the rope around Havick as he charges for me. Havick barges into the rope carelessly like it's a tripwire, pulling it taut until Grite is taken from his feet and forced to go along for the ride.

I hear Grite's shoulder dislocate as he's yanked into the open air by the anchor in his bicep. He crashes into Havick's back as I dodge all four of his fists and bind his legs with my rope like a lasso'd calf. I let go of the rope in time to duck beneath a loose arrow, grabbing a throwing knife from my thigh holster and flinging it in Lu Bu's direction.

I don't have time to see if I hit my mark as Osprey's talons dig into me from above. As much as I enjoyed winning against Ventur, I have no desire to be taken into the air for flight a second time. I grab a dagger from my waist and blindly slash at Osprey's right wing until it no longer has the strength to lift me. The oversized bird collapses to the ground atop me, shielding me from the sun's merciless rays.

I lay here for a second, enjoying my suffocation as I'm rewarded with rest.

Sloppy, Wisteria sighs as I gather myself. All of my enemies are downed. Havick and Grite are tied together like livestock at a rodeo. Lu Bu lays on her back with a throwing knife in her chest. Osprey twitches in pain as her carved wing does all it can to not fall from her body.

I have won.

Despite having the odds stacked against me, I have won.

What will you do when you face more than four enemies? Wisteria growls, unsatisfied with my performance. *What will you do in the heat of war when you're surrounded on all sides and your enemy keeps coming?*

"I'll continue fighting," I answer, my helm distorting my voice into a sound I've never heard.

Doubtful... Look at you. You can barely stand.

"I just need rest."

And rest you will, when your enemy kills you.

"I just won, Wisteria. I have nothing to prove."

You have everything to prove! The hellcat screams at me with frustration. *You are being sent into a den of vipers, Drakini! You saw what those Undead are capable of. Sure, you beat one of them by the grace of gods. But what will you do when there are 125 of them pitted against you? And now one of them harbors a vendetta against you. You disgraced Ventur... Do you think he will just accept the results of last night and roll over for you? Mark my words, that demon will kill you the next time he sees you, and this tournament will let him! All you've proven is that evil is real, and you've invited it to our doorstep. Will you be ready when it knocks?*

I shudder as my sweat turns cold. Wisteria is right. Whatever war is coming, it will have to wait. I've just started a war of my own, and it's against an enemy far stronger than myself. So what if I beat Ventur? I nearly lost my life in the process. A man like that can't go on knowing I live. He sees humans as little more than bloodbags. He won't settle for mediocrity, and he certainly won't tolerate letting me live with the secret I now hold. I embarrassed him, so he will make me pay for his own lack of humility.

Life was never like this in Fyrefell. It wasn't about who was the strongest or most powerful. We were a community, and we were strong because we stuck together. I stood up for Myre, not because I gained anything in the process, but simply because it was the right thing to do. We lived on principle, not power. It didn't matter how big or small, wealthy or poor I was.

For the first time since leaving, I suddenly miss the simplicity of it all. My father was right all along. I yearned for so long to see the outside world that I didn't cherish how perfect my life already was. Life outside Fyrefell always seemed like a treasure chest I didn't have the key to, so I spent my days lusting over the possibilities of what lay inside. But now I have the key, and now I've opened the chest, and now I see what's been inside this whole time. It was never treasure inside this chest; it was just an illusion of grandeur covering something much more dreadful.

"Let's run it again," I command, pulling my rope dart from Grite's bicep. The demonic man laughs away the pain and collects his swords once more. Osprey's wing heals as she takes to the sky. Havick beats his chest with his four fists. Lu Bu notches an arrow. At the flip of a dime, the pieces on this chess board have reset themselves, and war is ready for me once more.

Fight! Wisteria shouts.

17

NAP TIME

The few recruits who remain gather in the mess hall to receive news of what challenge awaits us. We are all going into the finals in the dark, and despite Garmin giving me inside information about the tournament's format, I still have no clue how this tournament will proceed.

I sit at an empty table near the back of the mess hall, furthest from the stage. I never made friends here, but even those who were once popular no longer fraternize with anyone. We are all each other's worst enemies. This tournament has taught us our opponents are the only thing standing between us and glory. And though we still have no idea what war awaits us, we do what we must to bolster ourselves in the selection process.

Everyone left is fighting for a spot in the Black Knights, this nation's elite fighting force recently brought by the Celestials as a gift for the merging of their empire with ours. Now that the Black Knights are no longer made up of solely Undead candidates, humans are eager to be embraced as this kingdom's first ever human Black Knight.

But not me.

The Black Knights don't fit my style of fighting. I tried to conform to their preferred weaponry—the sword and shield—but little good came from it. In fact, I'm not sure any of the recruiters have need of a warrior like me. The Marksman Corp is tailored to produce the kingdom's most lethal and accurate archers. The Mounted is only a step above the infantry. I've heard jokes going around that the only difference between an infantryman and a Mounted is that a Mounted gets to ride on a horse. The Rangers, dedicated to stealth and scouting seems like more of a fit for me, but I'm told by Garmin their recruiters are looking for fighters much quicker and agile on their feet than I.

Frankly, since the moment I learned they existed, my eyes have been on the Hunters. They are this kingdom's most elite and selective branch of the military, and they only have open spots when one dies or retires. In a world where humans must coexist with monsters, the Hunters are the ones that haunt those who haunt others. Undead, Lycan, human, the Hunters see no preference. When one of these three species goes off the rails and brings chaos, the Hunters are the ones who make them answer for their crimes. They are the ultimate system of checks-and-balances, and few know of their existence. Their work goes unapplauded and unappreciated, but that's just the way they want things. With the darkness as their ally, there is no monster safe from their judgment.

The only problem is... I don't know nearly enough about them to predict if I'm a fit for their forces. Nor do I know if their recruiter has been watching me all this time. If they don't have any spots open, I highly doubt they will care about this tournament other than to scout for future prospects.

I look back around me once more.

The few candidates that remain have all been invited to this dinner to enjoy one last meal before the final iteration of the tournament is revealed. In truth, I know I should be eating. Only Sylvian knows when the next time I'll have a warm meal put in front of me. But like everyone else around me, I just stare at my food and play with it. When nerves are high, my appetite disappears. There is so much for me to worry about. Even though I've made it to the final round of selection, there's no telling what waits for me.

And I, unlike those around me, know our Undead adversaries are awaiting our competition, and I know better than most that we humans are too weak to oppose them.

My thoughts are broken up as a young, nameless squire of the king clears his throat from the front of the mess hall. When he got here, I have no idea. He addresses us all in a booming voice, startling me due to the nature of his small body. "All of you must eat. The king has instructed your Arms Master he cannot instruct you on the tournament's proceedings until each bowl has been presented to the front of the mess hall empty."

And with that, the squire walks off and exits the mess hall from its front entrance.

Well, here goes nothing, I think to myself as I stare at the warm broth in front of me. Little chunks of meat and boiled dumplings float amidst green onions and potatoes. The cooks provided each of us with a relatively soft baguette meant for soaking up the soup. In essence, I eat this meal like it's a direct order from the king—my next battle in the tournament, except my rope dart and daggers have been replaced with a spoon and fork.

In less than a minute, I'm finished, and I mop up the remnants of broth with my bread. Everyone around me does the same, drinking the broth from their bowls like it is holy communion on the night of a lunar eclipse.

I stand quickly and bring my empty bowl to the front of the mess hall, stacking it atop those who've finished before me. Afraid of making eye contact with someone who wants my head on a pike, I move back to my seat with my eyes focused on my combat boots. Everyone here thinks very little of me. I am one of the only females remaining, and I am certainly the only warrior left who was in the bottom 500 rankings. Perhaps they think it's luck that's brought me this far. I don't see how that's possible, seeing that I have faced fighters exclusively ranked higher than me thus far, but so be it. In life, there will always be those who pray to see your downfall.

I sit, waiting for Arms Master Garmin Vaid to arrive with our marching orders.

And wait.

And wait.

And wait.

I drum my fingernails along the tabletop impatiently, wondering what could be taking so long. Then, without my permission, I yawn. I look around and see several other candidates resting their heads on the table. My eyes are getting heavy, like some unnatural force is trying to close them without my leave. What in the world is taking Garmin so long? Never once has he been the sort of man to arrive to his duties late. I'd like to think I know him better than most after nearly being killed alongside him, but maybe he's held up in the forge or some discreet meeting.

All around me, other candidates begin to yawn and rest their heads on the dining tables. Then, I hear snoring all of a sudden. That's odd, I think to myself. It's quite a queer time to be taking a nap, right when monumental information is about to be relayed to us.

Besides, if anyone deserves a nap, it's me. Wisteria has been working me tirelessly these past few days. What little sleep I've had was spent between sparring matches with her psychotic army of demons. I haven't seen a single one of these warriors pull an all-nighter on the practice fields. They've been sleeping each night comfortably away in their cots.

Now that I think about it, I do deserve a nap. I look around and see that everyone else is fast asleep around me. If I was in my right mind, I'd probably question how suspect these circumstances seem. But I am so tired. So damn tired. And my eyes are heavy. So damn heavy. I yawn again, then close my eyes and rest my head on the tabletop. I'm not going to sleep, I tell myself. I am just going to rest my eyes for a moment. But I won't let myself fall asleep. I won't let myself—

18

DO OR DIE

Wake up, girl! The tournament is beginning!

Huh?

I lift my head from my arms and stare at the long strand of drool that's glued to my forearm. I rub my fingers through coarse sand, but it isn't the sort I'm accustomed to from adding drainage back on father's farm. This sand is abundant, and as I look around at my surroundings, I realize it's everywhere—as far as my eyes can stretch. The noise of water crashes behind me, causing me to panic. I have never heard water like this before. It is not the incessant, ever flowing noise of a river.

I flip from my sand-covered stomach onto my backside as a wave washes around me, splashing over my feet and up to my waist. For a moment, I'm in too much shock to move. But then, as the saltwater retreats away from my soaking body, I relax.

I know where I am, but have no idea how I got here.

I've heard of this place before, though I never imagined I'd live to see the day I'd travel here in person. This is a beach—a place citizens of Fyrefell would talk about every once in a while. Their words, I now know, did it little justice. This place is like nothing I imagined could exist on earth. The sun sets over the water in the distance, casting its brilliant hues of fiery orange across the greenish blue waters.

"Where am I?" I ask no one in particular, mesmerized by the scene before me. Hard to believe most go their entire lives without ever seeing what nature displays before me this instant. At one point in my life, I thought I would be one of those people. Thought I would die in Fyrefell without ever seeing what this world has to offer.

Snap out of it, Wisteria growls, stepping in front of me with the hair on her back raised. When I lock gaze with her glowing yellow eyes, her look of urgency is enough to snap me out of my daydream. *This is life or death*, she asserts, calling my attention to my surroundings with a wave of her head. It isn't until now that I realize how confused I am. The last thing I remember is being in the mess hall, eating bread and soup until there was none left... Then, people started falling asleep around me... Then... What happened after that?

They drugged you, Drakini, Wisteria says as I come to the realization myself.

"Then... I..." I look around at the vacant beach as the next wave washes through Wisteria's translucent body and over my legs. "Where am I?"

The Skaarian Isles, Wisteria growls. *They took you and the other drugged up competitors and dropped you off on this island. Check your pocket. Garmin put a note in it when he left you here.*

How can this be? They drugged us and dragged us out to an island we know nothing about. To what? Fight each other? Finish off the tournament on a remote island where not even the recruiters can watch us perform? How does this make any sense?

I stand from the water as it retreats back to the ocean, reaching into my waterlogged pocket to retrieve a folded sheet of papyrus. Quite the lapse of communication, if I say so myself. Though I learned how to read in Fyrefell, how many candidates hail from provinces in this kingdom where they don't teach children simple reading skills?

I guess it's just another thing that gives me an edge in this competition. *Well? What does it say?*

"It says," I say, reading aloud, "Contestants. Welcome to the final portion of the tournament. You are in Skaar, an island off the coast of the Areopagan Empire. Skaar is home to one of this kingdom's greatest resources—silver. It's said the crashing of Phobos to earth is what splintered Skaar from the mainlands, and its surface is rife with ore for mining. In the past decade, though, a man by the name of Slave King Dyran has taken siege of the land and ceased all production of silver. Rather than sending an army to put an end to his tyranny, I have sent you—the final contestants in this draft's tournament. You will notice there are no recruiters here to watch you. That is because you are no longer being graded on your individual performance; rather, your performance as a unit overall. There are 500 of you in total, 125 of which are Undead recruits from the Northern military sector. A great military strategist once said, 'Only war can break all bonds of existing prejudice, because it is only during war that soldiers realize their differences aren't too great to overcome.' Despite the animosity between Undead and humanity, I expect you to work as a team to put an end to Dyran's rebellion. This is no longer a simulation. Your lives are on the line, and some of you will not make it back alive. The only ratings you receive will be those reported by your peers. Fail to make friends, and your rank will not be favorable. Die, and no one will remember you. Fail this mission, and we will carry on without you. Best of luck to all. Your King, Silenius Sylvian."

A team mission, eh? Wisteria growls, her tone suggesting she doesn't like the thought of that at all. *What about weapons? Did they think to supply all 500 of you with weapons?*

"It doesn't say anything about weapons," I reply, frustrated. This doesn't make any sense. Why is King Silenius treating this like some big game? If Dyran is actually a force to be reckoned with, Silenius wouldn't send 500 unarmed teenagers out here to deal with him. Or maybe, just maybe, this actually is just a big game to him. Silenius is only a teenager himself, and he only inherited the throne so early because his father was assassinated unexpectedly.

He is right though. We are being evaluated on much more than our fighting skills now. To survive this mission, we must learn to forage, to form teams, to work as a unit, and to accomplish a common goal. It would be a hard enough task if it was just us humans, but as soon as that sun goes down, the Undead will be here.

I've already had a taste of how they view humans, and it's not one I'm convinced will work in conjunction with fighting a war. The Undead know no such thing as teamwork. Even amongst themselves, they cannot agree. That is why they have factioned themselves into different tribes. Their pride is insufferable, and the odds of them working alongside us humans is lower than zero.

For some reason, I'm scared. This plan doesn't feel thought out. It feels like a child playing with his toys, sacrificing them like pawns to make a statement of power. Is Silenius Sylvian a tyrant in the making? Is he sane enough to inherit the crown? He has initiated the kingdom's first ever draft and forced us to train without disclosing what war awaits us.

"The sun is setting," I say, no longer mesmerized by the sun as it sinks on the horizon. I don't have the luxury of sitting on the beach and looking at its beauty any longer. Soon, blood will flow in these waters, tainting their beauty.

I was wrong earlier. Most go their entire lives without ever seeing what nature displays before me this instant, but maybe that isn't such a bad thing after all. If the price of traveling to see the world is war, maybe I was better off remaining in Fyrefell. But there is no time to regret my decisions now. All I can do is make sure it's not my blood that will soon taint these waters.

19

PRISONER OF WAR

Luna rises, calling her monsters of darkness to come forward.

I've retreated into a tropical jungle filled with plants and trees specifically unique to this region. Here, even the leaves are different. They aren't lush and plentiful like those that grow on trees in Fyrefell or Areopagus. They are sparse and sharp and cruel. These trees grow in a hostile environment, and they embody this hostility in their appearance. Some are carnivorous. I watched a plant swallow whole a mosquito the size of my fist. I've seen reckless birds be impaled by branches sharp enough to be mistaken for spears. Everything is different. The insects, the wildlife, the air. Noises fill the jungle's darkness with a mysticism enough to paralyze most with fear.

Not me though. With Wisteria's glowing yellow eyes to guide my way, she alerts me to dangers I can't see with my naked eye. Though she is a projection of my own imagination, she has abilities I don't. She is a hellcat, and her powers as a predator keep me on my feet. She can smell what I cannot, see what I am blind to, and hear so far in the distance that no one can catch me lacking.

Together, we are unstoppable. And with the help of my army of fictional characters, I traverse this land courageously. Osprey flies overhead, searching for other candidates and providing navigation to Dyran's whereabouts. Lu Bu scouts ahead, bow in hand, even though no one other than me can be damaged by her invisible arrows. Havick and Grite stick by my side, no longer my sparring opponents, but filling some role as motivational coaches as I carry on.

Skaar might be a remote island, but it is larger than I was led to believe. Osprey relayed it's broken into several islands, each of varying size and distance splintered through the ocean. The isle we candidates have been placed on is the largest of them all, amounting to approximately fifty kilometers across. It's a lot of ground to cover, but Osprey has spotted fires burning in the distance, signaling to me and Wisteria that it seems to be centered around a large rock quarry meant for mining.

If Dyran is anywhere, it will be where the silver flows like honey from a beehive, so that's where I head. In my hands are two wooden stakes I've broken off of indigenous trees. They required no whittling, because the trees here seem to sharpen themselves from the environment's adversity. Tucked along my thigh's holster are twigs durable enough and sharp enough to constitute throwing knives. I've been sent into war with no weapons, but I've turned nature into my weapon. I can only assume this is what King Silenius meant for us to do—another test on our survival skills as a soldier.

It's reminiscent of something a Ranger would do, turning their surroundings into an opportunity for lethality. We can only be as deadly as

our creativity warrants, so I let my creativity blossom. All I know is, if I
have a run in with Dyran's soldiers, or worse, an Undead, I don't want to
be caught empty handed.

Wings disturb the overhead canopy, causing me to tighten my fists and
ready myself to attack. I look up and breathe a sigh of relief, seeing it's
Osprey returning from patrol.

Purple eyes in sky, Osprey calls, landing on the sandy, loamy jungle floor.
Purple eyes with pale faces.

"Undead," I whisper to myself. "Are they headed for the mining quarry?"

No, Osprey replies, her voice shrill like a siren. *They are fighting one
another and hunting humans in the forest.*

"Figures," I sigh, twiddling my wooden daggers in my hand.

Let them come for small gorl, Havick bellows with laughter. *Small gorl
hurt them bad!*

Drakini'll turn their flesh into a hat and matching moccasins, Grite
laughs to himself. *Turn their bones into toothpicks!*

Someone's coming, Wisteria shouts, sprinting through the woods from
ahead. The terrain does little to affect her speed. She weaves in and out of
the trees and bushes, leaping like a pixie over downed trunks and between
briars with ease. *It's a human. The one you bested in battle before the tournament began.*

"Dante?" I question aloud. I walk quickly in the direction where Wisteria came from, then see him off in the distance, traversing the wilderness
like someone completely out of their element. His body shows signs of
weariness. His clothes are torn and tattered, as if he was dropped in some
briar patch and ripped apart by thorns. In his hand is a massive club the
size of my wingspan. He pants loud enough for me to hear from a quarter

kilometer away, and he makes enough noise to draw in an Undead from miles away. I reveal myself, then call his name in a shrill whisper.

He spins around, a panicked look on his face. His eyes dart across the surrounding jungle rapidly, trying to identify where the noise came from. This is not his element. Dante is a terrific warrior, but he is built for the arena, not for guerilla warfare.

He raises his club defensively, unsure of who calls him. I approach him with my palms raised, leaving the shadows of palm trees behind so he can see that I'm not a threat. We lock eyes from a few yards apart, and I watch relief wash over him. He sighs, lowering his club, "Drakini…"

"It's good to see a familiar face," I whisper, looking up to the sky for any sight of purple eyes. I see none, then proceed, "Are you alright?"

"Do I look alright?" he replies, laughing at himself with his arms spread to his sides. "Damn jungle has swallowed me whole and spit me back out. We haven't even been here a half day and I'm already hurting worse than the beating you gave me in the fighting ring."

"I think that's the point," I concede, finally verbalizing what's been bothering me all day. "They're testing us. They want to see how we cope in foreign environments. Thus far, they've given us everything we need to be successful. Weapons, food, shelter, training. But now, they want to peel us back like onions and see who can flourish when their back's against the wall."

"I fear the only thing that's flourishing on me is a bacterial infection from where the briars snagged me," Dante laughs, trying to minimize his embarrassment.

"You'll be fine. You have too big a body for infection to defeat," I reply coyly. "Have you run into anyone else out here?"

"Well, if by run into you mean discover their body mauled by a wild animal, then yes," Dante whispers, almost as if he's afraid the wild animal will hear him. "I guess a beast got to them before the drugs wore off."

"This is all so fucked up," I sigh in frustration. "I mean, what do they hope to accomplish by sending us all out here like this?"

"Like you said. It's a test. Separates the boys from the men, and I fear it's showing me how childish I truly am. Did you see that part in the note about the Undead?"

I try to hide the look of fear on my face. No one except me, Garmin, and Ventur knows I have already faced an Undead, but knowing 125 of them are here on this island is terrifying. "Yeah, I'm afraid so. Damn bloodsuckers are going to be more focused on us humans than they will be on taking down Dyran."

"If they were smart, they wouldn't. Night can only last so long. If they don't stay focused, they're all fucked when the sun rises. If I was them, I'd be flying to take down Dyran as we speak."

But they aren't, though I have no way to explain to Dante how I know this. Osprey's intel is enough to confirm my suspicions. The Undead are here, but their minds aren't focused on the goal we've been sent to achieve. Instead, they seek to test their hands against their human counterparts, to see which candidates are stronger than the other.

There is no rhyme or reason to their madness. They think they're better than us, but there's some insatiable voice in the back of their minds that compels them to prove it. The only way we humans will survive is if we stick together. If we don't—

A scream echoes in the distance. Dante and I look off through the woods simultaneously. At the same time, we inwardly compile everything we know about the victim's scream. It's a male, that much is evident from the voice. Likely human too, seeing there's no reason an Undead would shout for help when the night is their ally. And they are less than a hundred yards away, if we were able to hear them from here.

Drakini, don't, Wisteria growls. I look at her menacing yellow eyes through the shade of palm trees. If I listen to her, someone on my side of this war may die. There's no telling what peril has befallen them. Not until Dante and I go to investigate.

Dante takes off first, and I trail after him. This entire tournament, Dante has been like the knights I grew up dreaming about. Even when I faced off against him in the arena, he was caring and compassionate. He did not fight me out of rage or arrogance, but instead because it was his duty. He is chivalrous through and through, and I can't think of a better person to have on my team in a remote wilderness I know nothing about.

Grite and Havick remain by Wisteria's side, and Osprey no longer extends her wings to aid my mission. I look over my shoulder and see Wisteria's yellow eyes gleaming at me, disappointed in me for disobeying her orders. But I can't stop thinking about if it was me that needed help, and others ignored my call for it. We humans owe a duty to each other, even in the midst of this competition. There is no point in winning if it means sacrificing the souls of many.

I hear Wisteria growl solemnly as she whispers something under her breath. It sounds like she said, "Goodbye, brave child," but I can't be sure. I don't have time to weigh her words, nor will I turn around and beg for her companionship. She's a figment of my damn imagination, after all, but I can't let her orders overcome my morality.

My feet trudge through the loamy soil, leaping over roots and briar patches as Dante and I close in on the whimpering. Whoever is calling for help, their screams are not artificial. I can hear the pain, the agony in their vocal chords. But as Dante and I cross the tree line into an open valley of sand and rocks, I stop dead in my tracks at what I see.

Tied up between two posts is a human, and surrounding him is a band of Undead teenagers no older than myself. I swallow deeply as I lock gaze with a set of purple eyes, realizing I recognize his face. My stomach hurdles into my throat. Standing before me, assuming a position of authority over these Undead candidates, is Ventur.

"Well well well," Ventur laughs as Dante and I fall straight into his trap.

The human who is bound by the wrists and suspended by his own weight calls out to us, "I'm so sorry... They made me do it..."

His voice is oddly familiar, though I'm unsure why. The boy bound to the whipping post looks up at me through sweat-soaked bangs. I see the look of surprise in his eyes the same moment chills run through my body. "Myre?" I ask, my voice croaking with disbelief.

20

CRIMSON SAVIOR

"Drakini," he moans helplessly. I am overwhelmed with shock and grief and rage. I barely recognize Myre, not only because of the wounds on his body, but because his body looks nothing like it did when I knew him in Fyrefell. From head to toe, the boy I used to know is now covered with muscle only men possess. He no longer has a look of fear in his eyes, like he did when he clung to my side. Instead, his eyes are emotionless voids, like a dog that's had all the fight beat out of them.

I have no idea how he's made it this far in the tournament. This entire time, I've held him in the back of my mind, praying he wasn't killed by some savage foe the first round of the competition. Now my doubts are set aside as realization dawns—like me, Myre has figured out a way to make something of himself. Just as I am no longer the innocent girl he knew, he's killed and buried the boy I grew up with.

He had to, in order to survive. Still though, whatever he's done to evolve, it wasn't enough to save him from the horrors of this night. The Undead have him now, and only I possess the power to save him.

"That's enough out of you, bloodbag," a female Undead shouts, lashing his back with a whip made of braided bark and chipped rock. The rock cuts into Myre's flesh, causing him to cry out for help again as his blood spills beneath him. The female Undead walks up to him with her eyes on us, then licks the trickling blood off his back. It smears on her lips, then she exaggerates her movement as she licks her mouth clean.

If Ventur is afraid of me, he surely doesn't show it. He stares at me like he's never seen me before. Like we were summer lovers whose fling ended disastrously, so now he taunts me with his eyes because he knows the secret we share.

"I told you they would come, Celeste," Ventur snickers, gesturing at me and Dante. Suddenly, three more humans break through the woods on the opposite side of the clearing, and then it's too late. An Undead candidate lands behind them from the sky, shaking his head menacingly when they try to turn back. Another man, this one I recognize from the Western military sector, storms headfirst from the jungle to our right, thinking he is in the right for coming to rescue our belabored comrade. Like us, he is mistaken. And like us, he has fallen into this trap.

Several of the Undead laugh aloud. More and more humans enter the clearing, all of them just as confused as me and Dante. I bite the inside of my cheek each time a new face emerges from the shadows into the moonlight. I want to scream for all to hear that it's a trap. I want everyone who still rushes this way to turn back around. But if I do that, I may not make it out of here alive.

Damn me for not listening to Wisteria.

"So kind of you all to join us," Ventur shouts, his Undead troops moving in the shadows behind us so we have nowhere to run. He continues, "You humans, you're no better than the damn Lycans. Pack animals at the end of the day. How did I know that if I could get one of you to squeal, the rest of you would come running?"

"Because we actually care about our own species," Dante replies coldly, stepping forward into the night.

"Dante," I call after him in a hushed tone. He doesn't know what he's getting himself into. I've fought this demon before, and Dante doesn't have what it takes to counter his power. I look at my inferior, homemade weapons. Neither do I. If I try to fight Ventur like this, he will pulverize me with raw strength.

"Oh, what do we have here? A savant?" Ventur laughs, mocking Dante.

"Let us humans go," Dante orders. "We are all on the same side here. We all have the same goals."

"Oh, but I'm afraid we don't. You see, we Undead received quite an unsatisfactory final meal before being dragged out here. How could we possibly have the strength to take this island back for our king without proper nourishment?"

"There will be more than enough blood for your kind when we've defeated Dyran and his horde," Dante answers, not seeing that the question was rhetorical. "We are only wasting time and energy with these antics."

"We have all the time in the world out here, my dear... I'm sorry, where are my manners? I didn't catch your name."

"Dante."

"My dear Dante," Ventur finishes his sentence. "You see, we Undead don't care in the slightest if you humans make it back alive. If anything, our military will be better off without you. You're all nothing but a bunch of deplorable troglodytes. On the other hand, your king needs us Undead.

Why else do you think he formed an alliance with our tribes and brought us into the fold?"

"So we can make peace and put our pasts behind us," Dante answers naively. I cringe inwardly, not liking where this conversation is going.

"Stop playing with your food, Ventur," the woman named Celeste laughs.

"Come on guys, this isn't right," an Undead boy calls from the outer ring of warriors. "These humans are supposed to be our allies."

"Tsk tsk, Nikolai," Ventur growls, annoyed with his comrade's outburst. I recognize the latter's name. Nikolai... He's the second victor from the night Garmin and I spied on the Undead battles. The one who fought with the dual sided spear that detached in the middle. "Ever the human sympathizer, you've been. When are you going to realize they're food, not friends?"

Nikolai leaves the outer darkness and approaches Ventur candidly, as his equal. I bite down on my lip as the two stand eye to eye, neither one willing to bend the knee to the other. Nikolai replies, loud enough for all humans to hear, "You're wrong. We are the ones cursed by Damon. We are the ones who must consume blood to survive. Humanity has done nothing wrong to deserve this treatment."

"We consume blood because we are the next evolution in the food chain. The apex predators of this world," Ventur growls, his voice growing more frustrated each time he speaks.

"You sound like your father," Nikolai growls back, dissing Ventur in a way only Ventur can comprehend. "We aren't so different from them. It's time you put these primitive ideas behind you. This isn't 500 A.S. King Silenius brought us together like this because he believes we can be better than the stereotypes that got us exiled in the first place."

"Do you not see the difference between us and them, fool?" Ventur asks, then laughs again. "We Undead could fly away from this island right now if we chose to, and these humans would be stranded here until the mainlands decide to send boats for them. We stay because we want to. These humans stay because they have to. Every second we spend here is out of duty, not obligation. That is why *we* are the superior race, friend."

Ventur leaves Nikolai and approaches Dante. Suddenly, Dante no longer seems like such a daunting figure with Ventur standing beside him, circling him like a shark that's smelled blood. Ventur bends over and wafts Dante's neck, which provokes Dante.

"Get away from me, damn bloodsucker!" Dante rears back and readies his club in a defensive stance.

"See," Ventur says, eyeing Nikolai and gesturing to Dante. "You think we can coexist with a species that sees us as no more than bloodsuckers?"

"I—" Nikolai starts, but is cut off as Ventur moves through the shadows faster than Dante can react. I gasp in horror as Ventur closes the gap between him and Dante, then snaps Dante's neck. The perverted noise echoes across the clearing for all to hear. Dante's club drops from his raised hand, a look of surprise on his dead eyes as he falls to his knees, then plunges face first into the sandy soil.

"Stop!" I scream, sprinting forward.

Ventur looks up at me from Dante's corpse, his smile turning into a look of pure rage. A million unspoken emotions are exchanged between the two of us in less than a second. Time seems to freeze for the blink of an eye, and suddenly Ventur is on me, his palm closing around my throat faster than I can let out a scream for help.

Nikolai moves to help me, but several of his Undead companions cut him off, urging him to let Ventur do what Ventur desires most. My throat lets out nothing more than a gurgle as my feet lift from the ground. I plunge both of my wooden stakes into Ventur's sides, causing him to exhale with agony.

Unlike the wounds I gave him the last time we fought, these ones won't heal. My knowledge of the Undead is minimal, but Garmin taught me that they cannot heal from wounds inflicted by wooden stakes. It brings a twisted smile to my face, knowing Ventur will always have these stab wounds to remember me by.

"You cunt!" he screams, releasing me to retrieve the weapons I left in his ribcage. "Fucking wench, you're going to regret that!"

Ventur throws the wooden daggers aside and slams me into the ground, mounting me with my arms pinned down by his hands. I writhe in his grasp, shouting violently anything that will come to my mind. I scream for myself, but I scream also for Dante. This demon must be stopped. If no one else will stand up to him, I will do it for all of humanity.

I kick and claw and thrash in his grip, but it only makes Ventur laugh at me like I'm no more than a pathetic child. This angers me more, causing me to spit in his face and knee his hamstrings. I watch as my spit runs down his forehead, over the bridge of his nose, and atop his lip. He licks the saliva graciously, unfazed by my anger. Slowly, he bends down by my ear and whispers, "Not so tough now without your dagger on a chain, are you?"

"Fuck you," I growl back at him.

"Mmm, perhaps later, after I've drained you dry of all your blood," he sneers wildly.

"Unhand her," a hollow voice booms from off in the distance. I can't see who's arrived, but I can see from the perplexed reaction on Ventur's face it's not someone he expected. In less time than it took for him to snap Dante's neck, Ventur forgets I'm here. He stands from my captive body and stares venomously at his newest adversary.

I dust myself off and stare at the newcomer.

There, standing at the edge of the lethal jungle, is a tremendous knight covered head to toe in crimson armor, a bloodred sword in his hand ready to be tested.

"Oh look, another self-righteous oaf has come to die. What's your name?" Ventur asks, sneering violently. "I like to get to know my prey before I kill them..."

"King Dyran," the knight replies, his voice booming across the forest. He continues, "The man I'm assuming you've been sent here to kill."

21

THE MAN WHOM UNDEAD FEAR

The words sink in and all remain silent. Not even Ventur can think of a witty, smartass reply to that. Standing before us as my personal savior is King Dyran, the target we have been sent to kill, donning tight-fitting crimson armor from head to toe. It is unlike any armor I've seen before.

I still remember when knights first came to Fyrefell announcing the draft. Seeing them shocked me, as it was like the pages of a fable springing to life before my eyes. But this knight is different from those who came bearing news of the draft.

I've seen hundreds of knights since being drafted. I see them walking on patrol every day; I see them performing physical training early in the morning and I see them stumbling home drunk from the bars every night. This man before us—Dyran—is no knight.

He is a paladin. His armor is battle worn from what looks like decades of use, yet it gleams the reflection of the stars above. His helm is an intricate work of smithery not even Garmin would be capable of replicating. The only portion of his face left revealed is the slit where his dark eyes blend into the shadows within the helm. Intricate metalworking is welded like a production of nature, like the hairs atop a Lycan's head. There is no pivoting visor for him to reveal his face. The metal plating seems to be sewn and woven with hard, bloodred leather. The design the shape of his helm takes is that of a foul monster I've never seen before. From its temples sprout horns that resemble a rack of antlers. The faceplate itself is like the skull of some prehistoric creature long extinct. It is part human, part water buffalo, all gilded in red bronze to match the cryptic colors of his armor.

"You kids shouldn't be here," Dyran speaks sympathetically. "These woods are no place for people your age. This island is a sinister place."

"Then kindly hand us your head and we'll be on our way," Ventur quips back.

"I know what you're thinking," Dyran growls at Ventur as the Undead soldier stalks slowly toward him. "Don't try it. I have no interest in hurting a child."

"Don't belittle me like some infant! Could a child do this?" Ventur shouts, throwing his body through the air at Dyran faster than my eyes can track. I expect to hear the snapping of a neck again, followed by the thud of Dyran's body. Ventur moves impossibly fast, it's hard to believe anyone could see his attack coming. I've defeated him once before, but that was with weapons I've trained with and after Ventur had just competed in the tournament, and even then I only survived by the skin of my teeth.

I hear metal ring loud as Dyran's gauntlet makes contact with Ventur's face. My heart skips a beat as Ventur's speed meets an immovable object. Chills crawl down my spine at what I've just seen. Ventur's body hits the ground like limp noodles, fully unconscious from face planting into Dyran's fist. If only there were some way I could rewatch that scene unfold. Ventur is fast, but Dyran is somehow faster. One moment, he was standing with his arms by his side, sword in one hand, and the next, he was in a defensive position, swinging his fist to intercept his attacker.

I look at the faces of the other Undead soldiers. Each of them are equally, if not more, surprised than me. Celeste looks dumbfounded, like someone has just backhanded her with the knitted whip of sharpened rock in her grasp.

No one moves. We all just flitter our eyes between the knight and Ventur's cold, incapacitated body. Then I look at Dante—an entire soul of wasted potential. For some reason, the paladin reminds me of what Dante could one day become. A hero who stands up for those too weak to protect themselves. A knight in shining armor, like the ones in stories that make girls swoon. But Dante will never live up to any of this, because his dreams and future died with the snapping of his neck.

"Anyone else?" Dyran calls out, twisting his helm to look each of us in the eyes. Celeste's fingers dance along her whip's handle, making the chords dance in the sand with her body's nervousness. If she is smart, she won't try anything. The whip might have been effective on the Undead's prisoner of war, but it is a primitive weapon incapable of inflicting even a scratch on Dyran's armor.

Celeste looks around at her fellow Undead, the anticipation of the moment bottling up to the point of her screaming. "Are we just going to stand here? If we strike at once, this criminal can't stop us all!"

"Don't look at me," Nikolai sighs. He seems to be the most rational of the group.

"Why did you save me?" I ask, stepping forward into the night so Dyran can see me. "I mean, when he was on top of me... You told him to unhand me... Why did you do that? Why come here in the first place?"

Dyran half-looks at me, half-looks at Celeste while answering, not trusting her to stay put and keep her whip to herself.

"I heard that young man's scream for help, so here I am. As for saving you, I'm not sure what I did can constitute saving, but I've been on the receiving end of a few chokeholds before, so I figured I'd be a good distraction for you."

"How did you know we're here for you then?"

"I have eyes in the Areopagus, child. I never intended your king to get children involved with our affairs. I've done many things I'm not proud of, but killing children would be low, even for me."

"Why come to us then, if you know we are here to kill you? I mean, shouldn't you capture us as prisoners of war or something?"

"What use would I have for child slaves? No, ridiculous. I'm here to give you child soldiers a message to take back to your king."

"And what message is that?"

"Will you stop asking dumbass questions, human?" Celeste snaps at me. "Damon's sake, the man we need to kill is right there! We can have this whole mission done and over with and be in the Areopagus before the sun can even rise."

"It's only human of her to think before acting," Dyran replies, insulting the Undead to her face. "Humans aren't the impulsive creatures you Undead are."

"They aren't strong enough to be impulsive," Celeste sneers, getting into it with a man thrice her age. Dyran laughs at the response, almost as if he's enjoying this interaction. Such an odd shift of events. To go from hunting all night for this man to him coming to us. And now, we hold a casual conversation with him like we are villagers and he is our neighbor. How many conversations did I have in Fyrefell that felt like this? More than I can count, probably.

"Fuck this," Celeste grunts, twirling her whip behind her. "No one insults an Undead to their face without paying in blood." The knight looks unmoved by the threat.

"Don't make me hurt you," Dyran replies calmly, but it's too late. Celeste charges, lashing her whip in Dyran's direction. What she thinks her primitive weapon will do to this knight's armor, I'm unsure. But as Dyran moves to deflect the whip, Celeste releases it and leaps into the air. The attack was a diversion to get his attention off her real intent.

Celeste descends on Dyran as her Undead companions take this as their cue to move in on him like a vulnerable lion amongst jackals. Purple eyes lift into the air all around us like fireflies in the night sky. Almost as if they've synchronized their movements, they attack at the same time, easily outnumbering Dyran by a dozen. Nikolai, the human sympathizer, is the only one who doesn't make a move to attack Dyran. Instead, he stands idly by, watching his species devote themselves to something he doesn't believe in—needless bloodshed.

For a moment, I shrink back in fear. My battle trauma from Ventur makes me automatically assume Dyran stands no chance of conquering his foes. But as Dyran wields his sword like it's an extension of his body, I see this is a man well acquainted with doing what he must to survive. It is frightening to see how fast a man covered with armor can move. The armor does little to slow him as he jumps into action; it's like the metal plating is a second skin—an exoskeleton that boosts his strength and speed.

His sword is almost as long as I am tall, but he wields it effortlessly as he bats Celeste away with its broadside, almost like he is a batter at plate in a game of stickball. The sword makes contact with Celeste's midsection, cracking her ribs in the process. I revel in the sound of her shrieking in pain, yet I know she's just gotten off easy. Dyran's decision to strike with his sword's broadside was mercy, preserving her life instead of cutting her in half from hip to rib.

She is thrown from her flight and discarded to the ground like a rotten apple fallen from its tree. Dyran flips his blade around and buries his blunt hilt into the gut of an Undead traveling entirely too fast. The bloodsucker's momentum punishes him, causing his body to fold around the hilt, then collapse to the ground as the wind releases his flight.

With every move Dyran makes, I am making mental notes on how to make the Undead look foolish. Dyran slides to the ground as four Undead descend like lightning where he was standing. Facing flying opponents can be intimidating, but Dyran's style teaches me how to turn their flight into a weakness. Most of these Undead are unable to change their flight patterns at the drop of a copper. It isn't like running, where an athlete can cut quickly from side to side in order to change direction. When flying, the Undead take several seconds to divert direction whenever Dyran dodges their blows.

Meanwhile, Dyran moves fast enough to isolate his attackers, then subdues them while they're vulnerable. He catches the ankle of one as they descend on him, then places his hand on their back and capsizes their flight, causing them to flip midair and land face first on the ground. The impact is one that causes me to bite down on my tongue, and the Undead candidate doesn't get up after his fall.

Dyran kicks up sand into the eyes of one who charges him, causing the purple eyes to go temporarily blind. The bloodsucker's blindness makes him fodder for Dyran's reaping. Luckily for the Undead, Dyran is a merciful reaper. The crimson knight thrusts his knee into the bloodsucker's groin, effectively snapping the candidate's thigh bone in half. Not enough to kill, but definitely enough to dissuade the Undead from getting back up.

Two attackers team up on Dyran in sync, and Dyran makes them regret doing so in sync. He plants his blade in the pliable soil, then swings his body in their direction, a single hand holding onto the hilt, his metallic boots cracking each of them in their pale jawlines one after the other. The two attacked in sync, and they fall to the ground in sync.

During the heat of battle, Celeste has reclaimed her whip. She fondles her broken ribs as she sends it arcing for Dyran's body. Again, what she thinks her homemade lash will do against his impenetrable armor, I'm unsure. The shredded rock and glass hits its mark and wraps around Dyran's leg. Instinctively, Dyran stares at it, then follows the whip to its owner. Without hesitation, the knight severs the woven cord with his sword, then rips the portion of sharpened rock from his leg. The darkness of his visor locks on Celeste, and I linger in the look of fear that possesses her face. She no longer seems sure of herself as she watches Dyran wrap the whip around his fist so the rock and glass sits neatly atop his knuckles.

Celeste contemplates her odds, then decides she's ill-equipped and outmatched. With her ribs cradled in her hands, she leaps from the ground and takes flight into the night, leaving the wreckage she started behind. Those who joined her cause follow suit, flying above the tree line and as far into the atmosphere as they can. They are like children running from the boogieman, and all that remains in their wake is several unconscious Undead and Nikolai, who holds his hands up open-palmed as a sign of surrender.

Dyran doesn't so much as pant from the exertion of battle. If anything, he made this fight look like an effortless warmup. Whatever it is he's been through, whatever training regimen prepared him to fight like this, it makes me swoon like some fangirl.

Ever since my father's death, I've abhorred knights. Ever since they pinned me to the ground and violated me sexually, I've developed a subconscious hatred for them that knows no bounds. But now, after meeting the man I've been sent here to kill, my hatred falters, dwindles. This is not a man who uses his position of power to subjugate those inferior to him.

From what I can tell so far, Dyran is actually chivalrous, like the knights mother once told stories about. He is not a man I wish to kill at all, not that I think I am strong enough to do so even if I wanted to. This is the sort of man I want to learn from, not fight against. I stare at those he fell in battle. Not a single one of them is dead. This fight is not one he wanted to partake in, but even as these bloodsuckers attempted to kill him, he showed mercy in pulling his punches.

Without speaking, Dyran approaches the whipping post where Myre shivers in fear. Dyran cleaves his sword with deadly accuracy, severing the rope that binds him to the post. The boy drops to his knees, showing us his lacerated back. Celeste's whip has eviscerated his flesh, the sharpened rock and glass attached to its end opening him up enough to expose muscle and bone.

"We must treat your wounds, child," Dyran announces. At his feet, the boy trembles from fear and adrenaline. Though we had to be thirteen to be eligible for this draft, Myre's wounds make him look younger than ten. His injuries are severe enough to keep him curled in a ball on the ground. But Dyran bends over nonetheless and picks him up, slinging him over his shoulder like he weighs no more than a sack of potatoes or barley.

Dyran turns to us humans who lurk in the shadows, silently aware he's the only reason blood still flows through their veins. "Those who wish to live may follow. Those who want my head on a pike, let these Undead serve as a warning."

And with that, he disappears into the woods without another word. I hover over Ventur's sleeping body for a moment, wondering if the world would be better off if I ensured he never woke again. But after seeing what I've just seen, I'm inspired by Dyran's chivalry, then realize there's no honor in slicing open a sleeping throat. My time with Ventur will come, but until then, I will follow Dyran.

22

THE BLOODBAG FARMER

"You don't think it's just a little bit crazy that we're trusting this man after watching him pummel fellow candidates into the ground?" Nikolai asks in a hushed voice as we trek through the wilderness to keep up with Dyran.

"Your friends had that belliwhopping coming," I answer, still not used to the fact that I've somehow adopted an Undead as a companion.

"Friends is an awfully strong word," Nikolai laughs. "Even acquaintances would be pushing it." Checks out. Nikolai is nothing like the other Undead I've interacted with. When the rest of his species stood ready to attack us humans, Nikolai was the only one with balls big enough to face Ventur down. Yet at the same time, Nikolai did nothing to get Ventur off me before Dyran showed up, and he did nothing to help Myre as his back was flayed open.

"I saw you stand up against Ventur when he was calling for our blood. Why did you do it?"

"It just seemed like the right thing to do... You don't know Ventur, he would have slit your throats and collected your blood in conch shells to drink..."

"I know him better than you think," I reply, trying to keep my voice steady as I fight to hide my labored breathing. Now's not the time to tell Nikolai I already fought Ventur. That's information I can't entrust with anyone I just met, so I let the statement linger. "He's the same as all you bloodsuckers. The Curse of Damon plagues his heart."

"Hey, watch who you're calling bloodsucker, warmheart. Do you think I asked to be like this? You think I enjoy my insatiable appetite for human blood?"

"There's a million different animals that have blood you can suck on. Why you Undead have to target humans is beyond me."

"Nor would I expect you to understand," he says defensively, "But can't you just put yourself in our shoes? Damon's Curse is a hunger. It claws at our guts night and day, Drakini. The only thing that can remotely dull its pain is blood consumption, but not all bloods are equal. Trust me, don't you think we've tried sustaining ourselves on the blood of other mammals? I myself have drank deer, rabbit, cow, chicken... Hell, I've even chewed fish guts! Nothing comes remotely close to filling the void we feel. Only the blood of a human can do that."

"So what, you Undead just expect us to bend our napes for you until the end of time so you don't have to bear your tummy aches?" I ask, inflecting my tone so he knows I am judging him.

"Not everything has to be so black and white, you know?" Nikolai defends. "Whether you like it or not, our empires are merging. We will soon go to war together, and it's up to us to be open-minded. Besides, bending the nape is such a dramatic phrase. If every human under Silenius's control willingly donated blood, the Undead would have enough to live on for centuries."

"And what would we humans get in return? Huh? What valuable resource is your empire providing us humans to pay us back? Because all I've seen so far is Undead like Ventur doing everything he can to prove why you're all unworthy to receive our blood."

"You're not going to catch me defending Undead like Ventur and Celeste, but a few bad apples don't define a species. Surely there are thousands of humans out there that you wouldn't want to define your character."

The image of a human knight pinning me to the ground to violate my body flashes in my mind. Not just one, but multiple. They took turns perverting the holiest part of my virgin body. They treated me like an object, not a fellow human. What they did, in many ways, was worse than an Undead feeding on a human's blood. At least that is justified—an Undead needs blood to survive, and like Nikolai said, he didn't ask to be cursed by Damon. What the knights did to me in Fyrefell, though... There was no purpose there. They had no need to rape me. Their survival wasn't at stake. They did it simply because they wanted to, and they did it because I was too weak to stop them.

I wouldn't want humanity to be judged off the actions of cowardly men like that, which makes Nikolai partly right. I didn't ask for this merger between our nations, but I am powerless to prevent it. For the foreseeable future, I will have to serve side by side with Undead. And with war on the horizon, it's looking like this will be more time than I anticipated.

"Why do you think no one else joined us?" I ask, disappointed by my fellow humans for staying back.

"For the same reason I just said," Nikolai replies. "It's a little bit crazy that we're trusting this man after watching him single-handedly battle a dozen Undead."

"It doesn't strike you as odd that he didn't kill a single one of them?"

"This whole situation strikes me as odd. I mean, the man is literally saving a human who was sent here to kill him."

"And yet, I'm the only human who chose to follow him."

"At least you weren't dumb enough to try to kill him. I'm never letting Ventur live down the moment he was defeated by a human, after all the bragging he's been doing since the draft started." Hearing this makes me want to spill the beans that Dyran isn't the first human to best Ventur, but I bite my tongue and decide to drop the subject.

"What makes you so different from the others? I mean, wouldn't it have been easier to go along with Ventur instead of defying him?"

"There's nothing easy about the politics that come with being Undead. Just look at us, even after being exiled, we couldn't stand united. Our belief systems and worldviews are a product of thousands of years of stubborn hatred for the circumstances our species faces. At least Lycans are smart enough to know there's strength in unity. We couldn't even acknowledge that. Ventur is the way he is because his father is Tribe Celestial's Count. It's essentially the same role Silenius plays for Areopagus—a monarch of sorts. I've known Ventur since I was a child, and I've watched him become the man he is today. Being the son of a Count comes with pressure, and I fear it's done more harm to Ventur than anything.

"I, on the other hand, was raised by bloodbag farmers. We are Tribe Celestial's biggest provider of blood, the ones who breed humans to ensure our society always has lifeblood to consume."

"Wait, you mean to tell me that's a real thing? I mean, I heard rumors about it, but I thought it was just some kind of exaggeration! You enslave humans like livestock?" I ask, enraged by the idea.

"These humans are by no means slaves. They come to us voluntarily, and we reward them for their sacrifice. To ensure a clean, quality flow of blood, we have to nourish them properly and provide for their needs. A human has all they could ever want when they live on a bloodbag farm."

"What do you mean they come to you voluntarily? What kind of person would want to live like that?"

"You'd be surprised. This world is a harsh place, Drakini. Giving a little blood to us Undead in exchange for a pampered lifestyle is ideal to many humans. They don't have to work, they don't have to hunt, they don't have to search for shelter. All of it is provided to them by us."

"You're crazy if you think I'm buying that narrative," I reply, scoffing at the idea of humans willingly feeding an entire population of Undead just because it gives them a cushioned lifestyle.

"Believe what you want, but it's true. And it's the reason I'm different from Ventur and the others, to answer your question. Bloodbag farmers are the only ones in our society that interact with humans. It's our job to make sure they are happy enough to remain with us, and it's our job to ensure those who stay are happy enough to produce offspring for the next generation. Unlike Ventur, I know many humans. Before the draft, I tended to them every day. Like the Undead, some of them are awful, entitled pieces of shite. But it's easy to overlook the few bad apples when there are so many that are kind and caring. That's how I know the other Undead will come around. The more time they spend with humans, the more they will see how wrong they are. Humans are responsible for our exile, so our forefathers have taught us to hate you. But in time, they will see there is nothing at all to hate."

"Or they will assume positions of power and try to take over our kingdom," I reply, believing this a much more likely outcome than the Undead learning to coexist.

"As long as there is a Sylvian on the throne, that will never happen," Nikolai dismisses immediately. "The only pride bigger than Ventur's is a Sylvian's."

"I don't know much about the Sylvians," I admit aloud, not wanting to announce my ignorance but knowing I should learn about our kingdom's leader sooner than later. "I never had to before the draft. All that mattered before this was surviving to the next day."

"And those survival instincts have served you well, it looks like," Nikolai says, gesturing at the jungle around us. "You've made it to the final 500 candidates, and you've found the man we've been sent here to kill."

"Yet I don't want to kill him, nor do I think he should die."

"There's much we don't know. After all, we weren't aware of this mission until we were drugged and thrown on this island like a poorly executed experiment. Like I said, a king has politics to think about. Dyran has single-handedly stopped the production of silver in Skaar, the largest producer of silver this nation has. Without it, many things have ceased. Weapons, currency, infrastructure, development. But worse than this, it's made Silenius look weak. He's only just ascended the Areopagan Throne, and already he has an entire island rebelling against him. It's not a good look for a teenage king who's being circled by sharks for a position of power. I don't envy the king. He's the same age as us and he already has more enemies than friends. I didn't ask for the Curse of Damon, and Silenius didn't ask to be king. He was born into this role, and so he's dealing with the cards he's been dealt."

"He has an entire battle-hardened army he could have sent, but he sent 500 teenagers instead. What kind of sense does that make?"

Nikolai laughs. "I'd be lying if I pretended to have an answer when I've been wondering it myself. It's a queer place to send your army's next generation of talent, that's for sure. Maybe it's a test, maybe it's straightforward. What the hell do I know, I'm only a bloodbag farmer at the end of the day."

Still though, as I watch Dyran saunter through the woods ahead of us with Myre's unconscious body slung over his shoulder, I can't help admiring what he stands for. He is saving the life of a complete stranger. Without immediate medical help, Myre would die from the infection coming for his wounds. *Maybe it's a test*, I repeat Nikolai's words inside my head. It leaves me thinking—what sort of test could a child pass that an adult couldn't?

And that's when I find the answer I've been looking for.

"I don't think we're here to kill Dyran after all," I whisper to myself, loud enough for Nikolai to hear.

"Dyran," I shout, rushing to catch up to him. "You said you want us to bring back a message to our king. What message were you talking about?" Anxiety and adrenaline rushes through my mind as I come within a wingspan's distance of the crimson knight.

"There's much you don't know about this world, child. I will teach you once we've reached my healer," Dyran's voice booms.

"But what if there's been some kind of miscommunication?" I ask, trying to parse through my endless thoughts to relay my epiphany. "What if King Silenius didn't send us here to kill you?"

"Obviously he didn't send you here to kill me," Dyran says. "No offense to you, but my army and I have over thirty years of military experience. To send children here to fight us is asinine."

"Exactly what I was thinking," I agree, then follow up, "But what does Silenius really know about you?"

"What do you mean?" Dyran grunts, hacking away a grove of briar vines with his tremendous sword.

"Does he know you are compassionate?" I ask, then follow up, "Would he know you're the kind of man who wouldn't kill children?"

Dyran pauses in his footsteps unexpectedly, almost causing me to run straight into him. I hear him whisper under his voice, "Shit." A wave of urgency takes over Dyran as he realizes what I have. He takes off running, knowing there isn't a moment to waste. I take off after him, and Nikolai calls after us, "What in Damon's name are you two talking about? Why are we running!"

We leap over fallen logs and arching roots. Our feet send up sandstorms with every stride. Dyran is fast—wicked fast. For a man wearing a full suit of armor, I can't imagine how much faster he'd be in just his flesh. I can barely keep up with him now. He knows this jungle like the back of his hand, and each step he takes seems like he's taken it a thousand times before this night.

I see Wisteria's eyes off in the distance, always watching like amber on fire. She's mad I didn't listen to her, and I fell into a trap that nearly killed me because of it. But if I had obeyed her order, I may have never met Dyran, and I sure as hell wouldn't have seen him belliwhop Ventur's brigade. Wisteria can be mad at me all she wants, but I'd be lying if I said seeing her eyes in the distance didn't provide me comfort. Without her, I feel weak. She is the only thing that's changed in my life since I realized my strength, and I wouldn't have realized it without her. So long as I know she's nearby, my strength endures.

Still though, I've grown so used to her company that I almost feel lonely without it now. And she's recalled my shadow soldiers—Havick, Grite, Lu Bu, and Osprey—imaginary friends whose absence sits heavy on my heart. It feels weird to say I'm incomplete without the figments of my imagination. It feels weirder to admit that when I'm in the presence of two living beings. I can't let it affect my judgment, and I sure as hell can't let it convince me I'm weak.

I've proved myself over and over. No need to let Wisteria's distance convince me I'm lesser without her. My father's words echo in my head—*Men are strong. Women are weak. It's the way the gods made us. If you join this draft, you will die before you ever see war. Men will put you in the dust and trample over you.*

Perhaps somewhere, my father is out there looking over me, and I am showing him how wrong he was. Men may be strong. Women may be weak. It may be the way the gods made us. But it isn't the way we have to remain. With enough training, a woman like me can defeat a man like Ventur. And with even more training, a man like Dyran can lead a rebellion against an entire nation.

As we break free of the jungle, Dyran's arm clotheslines me. My sternum runs right into his armored elbow, knocking the wind out of my lungs. I stumble backwards, hitting Nikolai as he rushes headfirst from the jungle behind me. Him and I collide, falling together in a twist of limbs and muffled grunts.

"Fuck's sake," Nikolai mutters as we rehab our dignity. I can't believe Dyran's arm was strong enough to stop my full momentum. Hitting his arm felt like running into a brick wall. He didn't even flinch, and now that I look beyond his body, I'm glad that he didn't. A few feet in front of him is the edge of a cliff with a drop off steep enough to paint the ground below with my brain splatter.

I stand, gathering myself to peer off in the distance. My heart sinks as I confirm my suspicion.

What sort of test could a child pass that an adult couldn't?

That's what I asked myself moments ago, and that's what led me to this epiphany.

Why send 500 child soldiers to an island led by a man who won't kill children as an act of war?

"We were a distraction," I whisper to myself as dread floods my heart. Off in the distance is a crater home to Skaar's largest silver mining operation, Dyran's homebase on the island. Dyran stands in vehement silence as he takes in the news I wanted to warn him of. Scattered across the crater before us is fire, and amongst the fire is more than a hundred blinking purple eyes.

In less than a single day, Silenius has retaken the island Dyran has held for nearly a decade. Using tournament candidates from the draft to draw Dyran out, Silenius has sent an actual army of Undead to seize back Skaar's silver mining operation, effectively defeating Dyran in one fell swoop.

Screams erupt and echo across the crater's floor. Dyran's soldiers that remain do all they can to fend off the attacking Undead, but the purple-eyed army is relentless. Dyran's forces may have over thirty years of military experience, but the Undead outnumber them five to one. To the bloodsuckers, this is a hunt for their next meal.

"Holy fuck," Nikolai gawks beside me, taking in the destruction that ensues. "Silenius has sent Tribe Celestial to take back the mines..." The information hits Nikolai harder than myself, seeing these are his people.

Though I don't know nearly as much about the Celestials as Nikolai, the sparkling silver hair is enough to indicate the truth of his statement. Everything Nikolai preached to me about coexisting previously has now been thrown out the window. As I watch the Undead descend on men and women fending for their lives, I clench my teeth and ball my fists. Dyran's soldiers let out involuntary screams as Undead gouge their fangs into their victims' necks.

"That bastard," Dyran whispers under his breath. Everything's changed now. "He has no idea what he's just done."

"Oh, on the contrary," a voice calls from behind us. Dyran is somehow able to spin around before me and Nikolai both. Though I can't see the expression beneath his helm, I can tell Dyran is not used to being caught off guard. As Nikolai and I spin to face our successful stalker, the voice continues, "I think I know precisely what I've just done."

"King Silenius," Dyran growls, raising his sword as I lock eyes with a somber boy with silver eyes.

23

THE CHILD KING

"Put the sword away, Dyran. I'm not here to fight you," Silenius says, waving his hand dismissively.

"My people are dying down there!" Dyran sneers, lowering Myre from his shoulder onto the ground. "You conniving serpent, you baited me away from my domain with quarreling children! What kind of coward are you?"

"A clever one," Silenius replies. "One that has your best interests at heart, believe it or not." I am too stunned to speak. Here I am, caught deep in a woven web of treachery and lies, unsure what to think or believe. Hours ago, I thought this competition was as simple as killing a rebel for the chance at elevated military status. Now that Silenius is here, I know much more is at play.

I look into the sparkling silver eyes of a boy no older than me. He is handsome, devilishly handsome. With a lean face set behind unkempt black hair, he looks like a demented angel. Thanks to Garmin's expedited teaching of history, I have learned Sylvians possess the power of both the Undead and Lycans, both accessible to them at any time and place. This makes them superior to even the Undead. Like the Undead, Sylvians can fly, but unlike the bloodsuckers, Sylvians can walk in the daylight without burning, and they don't need to feed on blood to be sustained.

Even more, Sylvians can call on the Curse of Dagon to morph into a wolf-like demon whenever they want. But unlike Lycans, the beast doesn't control a Sylvian's actions. Where all Lycans fall victim to the beast within on the night of the full moon, a Sylvian can call on their beast at any time and still hold the reins over their mortal body.

Sylvians are two beasts in one, a complex dichotomy of power and ferocity. There are likely a million ways Silenius Sylvian could kill Dyran right now, yet he opts for a conversation over conflict. What the fuck is happening? The king of Areopagus and all fiefs within its domain is standing before me staring down the point of Dyran's sword, and he's calmer than Ventur's unconscious body!

"Explain yourself!" Dyran shouts, his voice shaking with unconsolable rage. I must admit, I feel for the crimson knight. Silenius has played him for a fool and used the knight's chivalry as a weapon against him. Now, there's no telling how many innocent lives die beneath us at the hands of purple-eyed bloodsuckers.

"For years, you sent messengers to my father Salvador Sylvian. For years, he didn't respond. Salvador is dead now. I sit on the throne, and I am here to hear you out," Silenius says, no emotion in his voice.

"And you had to slaughter my entire army just to hear me out? Don't you have any idea what's down there? Don't you have any idea what you've just unleashed?" I can hear the sadness in Dyran's voice. He sounds as if he's on the brink of tears. Thirty years he's known those soldiers on the ground. Thirty years of camaraderie, thirty years of companionship, thirty years of brotherhood, all extinguished in a single night.

"I've read all the messages you sent my father, and I'm hoping that means I know exactly what's down there."

Nikolai and I feel like awkward bystanders caught between two ex-lovers in the middle of a public spat. To make this worse, neither of us has any idea what the fuck these two are talking about.

Dyran continues, "Then you know that your little posse of Celestials are about to set free a magnitude of evil this continent has never seen before?"

"I just said I read your letters, didn't I?" Silenius asks rhetorically. "Do you think I'd come here personally, unescorted, if I didn't believe you? No one knows I'm here, not even the Celestials that raid your operation. I had to orchestrate all of this to deceive those who plot in the shadows. I think it'd be best if we continued this conversation without any witnesses, wouldn't you agree?" Silenius gestures at me and Nikolai, looking over our existence like we are flies on the wall.

"You're the reason these children are here in the first place," Dyran laughs scornfully at Silenius's request. "Their lives are now at stake because of you, so I'd say they have just as much a reason to hear your explanation as I do."

"What I wish to discuss is classified," Silenius rebuts, "And it has a great deal to do with Tribe Celestial. I can't possibly divulge my intentions in the presence of one of their pupils." Silenius nods his head at Nikolai, not even bothering to look my Undead companion in the eyes.

"Wait, no," Nikolai counters. "I'm not like them," Nikolai says defensively, pointing out at the crater filled with monsterish purple eyes. "I've hated this curse my entire life. It's done nothing but bring me suffering. I'm telling you, whatever you have to say about my species, it stays with me. If you hate them, I can promise I hate them more. The day I received news our tribe would be merging with your empire was the best day of my life. Not because I wanted fame or status, but because it was finally an opportunity to prove myself, to prove I'm more than this curse in my veins. You have to believe me, King Silenius. I won't ruin this second chance you've given me."

"It's true," Dyran confirms. "I overheard the boy speaking this way in confidence to the girl. He means what he says." My face reddens as I realize Dyran could hear me and Nikolai's conversation the entire time we hiked to this cliff's edge. How many things did we say about him that would incriminate us? I want to rack my brain but the seriousness of this moment doesn't allow it.

Silenius sighs, then smiles. "So be it, we don't have time to bicker over who gets to hear our bickering." I watch a wave of relief wash over Nikolai. In a single breath, the Undead has spilled a lifetime of emotion from his heart. I didn't know before if I could trust him, but now I know there's few I could trust more than him.

"Count Viren of Tribe Celestial assassinated my parents," Silenius announces, his face unflinching as he throws everything I know into a whirlwind of confusion. The statement is enough to make Dyran lower his sword back to his side. Nikolai's pale face looks as if it's just been slapped. Silenius continues, "Very few know the truth, but I am one of those few. Many conspired for my father's throne, but it was only Count Viren who figured he could take it without ever having to wear a crown."

"It... It can't be," Nikolai stammers in disbelief. But as I look at Nikolai's face, I can tell he knows the truth deep down. Nikolai has known Ventur his whole life, which means he has personal experience dealing with Ventur's father. Nikolai said it himself, being the son of a Count comes with pressure, and it's done more harm to Ventur than anything. I've seen enough of the Undead to know their leader is capable of committing such an allegation.

"Yet it is," Silenius confirms, mourning his parents' deaths with a single exhale. Since coming to Areopagus, I always heard rumor about the suspicious circumstances surrounding King Salvador's passing, but I never knew the truth could be so grave.

"The entire merger of Undead into the Areopagus's populace was fabricated. It's all a farce. A well-executed plot by Viren to get his people out of exile and into the limelight. And now, as a self-nominated member of my council, he influences my reign of this kingdom through fear. What I'm saying to you must never leave this place. What's been set in motion cannot be stopped. For me to undo the merger between our species would result in the death of civilization as we know it. Now that they've sank their fangs into our society, they will tear open our carotid if we try to remove them."

"So you sent them here to die," Dyran jumps ahead of Silenius, guessing his strategies.

"I sent them here to get their damn eyes off me," Silenius scoffs. "And yes, if a few hundred of them die at the hands of this monster you wrote about to my father, then so be it. I know it was cruel to send teenagers here, and I know it's cruel that your people die at the hands of Undead as we speak. But believe me, this was the only option I had. Viren watches everything I do, every move I make. So I had to ask myself... What does an Undead care about more than power?" Silenius lets the question hang in the air for us to contemplate.

"Silver," I answer, the sound of my own voice startling me.

"Precisely," Silenius says. "You've shut down Areopagan production of silver for nearly a decade in order to get my father's attention, but your strategy was all wrong. The Sylvians have no need for silver, because we aren't the ones who fear Lycans. The Undead though... They need silver. They need silver like they need blood. The Lycan is their mortal enemy, and without silver to forge their weapons, there's nothing protecting them from the cursed hellhounds knocking on their doors. That's when I crafted this plan, Dyran. A way for us to kill two birds with one stone, if you will. You finally get an answer from the king you've petitioned for ten years, and I get your help in getting the Count off my back so I can fix the mess he's created. But I knew pitching this idea to the council would be difficult, so I went into your military records, and that's when I fell down this rabbit hole...

"You are not a rebel," Silenius announces, staring at Dyran's eyes through his hollow visor. "You're a damn hero, that's what you are. I may be a child in your eyes, but sometimes it takes a child to see things as they are." Dyran does little more than stand silently as the compliment washes over him. Silenius alternates his eyes between me and Nikolai as he continues, "Nearly twenty-five years ago, just five years into this man's military service, my father sent a portion of his military overseas to search for foreign land. On those boats was Dyran, a candidate in a now extinct branch of military known as the Conquerers. Their mission: Find new land and expand the Areopagan Empire.

"And find new land they did, but in this land was a creature they discovered unlike any this world has ever seen. The files have been classified since they crossed my father's desk, but those who know of this land's existence call it the Deadlands."

"There's no amount of reading records that could have revealed to you the hell on earth I discovered," Dyran growls, almost offended Silenius would even speak on the existence of the Deadlands. Something twists inside me—almost like I'm excited. The king of this nation has just confessed there is even more out there in this world to be explored. My whole life, I thought all there is exists between the Areopagus on the east and the Thoren Mountains on the west.

"Fifteen years you were trapped there," Silenius continues, ignoring Dyran's outburst. "Fifteen years you survived on this hostile terrain. You and your fellow Conquerers were declared missing in action, and your deaths were assumed publicly after five years passed without your return."

"Your father sent no rescue team! He left us there to die like fucking animals," Dyran accuses, his chivalrous nature dissipating as the traumatizing memories set in.

"My father is dead," Silenius replies. "If you have complaints with his decisions as king, take it up with his grave. However, I'm king now, and I have heard your call for help. You've done everything in your power to get my attention, so I'll do everything in my power to meet your demands."

"You can't be serious..." Dyran gasps, fumbling for an accurate response.

"Ten years you've demanded for the king to send an army to the Deadlands under your command. Tonight, you have my promise I will provide that army, provided you kill Count Viren by the time the sun rises."

"What creature are you talking about?" I interject, unable to let the thought linger long enough for an answer. "You said a creature inhabited the Deadlands unlike any this world has ever seen... What was it?"

"Stick around and you might find out," Silenius laughs. "Seeing our friend Dyran here has brought one back from the Deadlands and trapped it in the mining shafts."

"You really mean this?" Dyran asks, weary of where the king's loyalty lies.

"I'm staking my life on this gamble," Silenius says, his face unmoving. "I couldn't be any more serious. Now, do we have a deal?"

24

VERE MORI SKATHEN

"Are you two sure you want to go through with this?" Dyran asks me and Nikolai.

"Regardless of how many times you say it, we aren't children," I answer. "We're both sixteen, and we've trained for this tournament tirelessly. We can do this."

"Okay," Dyran agrees, reassured. He knows he needs us if we're to get Count Viren separated from his company. The host of Undead is too large for Dyran to take on himself, but with our help, we can set up the perfect trap for him.

"Like Silenius said, the goal is for the monster to kill the Count so his death looks like an accident. For that to happen, we need you to draw him in, Drakini. I hate to put you in harm's way, but Viren is known to like his blood from younger humans. You need to understand that this man is a predator, but what I have trapped inside these mines is an apex—something from the Deadlands that hunts and kills Lycans and Undead for sport.

"Nikolai, you'll help set the trap. After the pieces are in place, get Drakini the hell out of there. Once the Count is trapped and the mines are opened, there's no telling what madness will unfold. Then, it will be up to the Undead to kill the monster."

"What is this thing?" I ask, trying to imagine a beast capable of hunting both Lycans and Undead. "If this thing doesn't have the Curse of Damon or the Curse of Dagon, and if this thing isn't a Sylvian, then how can it be powerful enough to take on an army of the Undead?"

Dyran stares at me through his hollow visor, deep in contemplation. Fifteen years he was trapped in the Deadlands. Fifteen years he saw unspeakable things he's unwilling to share. It's in these fifteen years he developed his superior fighting skills, forced to fight for his life from day to day. It was in this time Dyran learned there is a beast far more sinister than Lycans and Undead, and the newly discovered beast ravaged the wastelands, consuming any living being that crossed its path.

"The Deadland natives have a name for it," Dyran says softly, his voice suddenly somber. "They called it the Wendigo—'an evil spirit that devours all.' The natives have their own mythologies for how it came to be, but the common consensus among them was simple... The Wendigo was the Creator's attempt to make a being capable of hunting the offsprings of Luna and Solis to extinction. The natives worshipped its existence like a god, but it is anything but that. It symbolizes winter, represents hunger, and embodies selfishness. There's no single consensus on its origin, but the natives believe the Wendigo's powers were a gift from the Creator to humanity as a way to fight back against their oppression.

"All I know is what I've seen in person—the Wendigo's bite can infect humanity. It is like a plague that spreads in their veins. It turns them into a monster, one much worse than a Lycan or Undead. It creates within them an insatiable hunger for flesh. To be Wendigo is to forever be hungry. But even worse, it changes a human's appearance into a personification of something truly evil. I've seen a Wendigo tear a Lycan in half at the waist; I've seen it take on an entire village of Undead. They have no known weaknesses, and they have no known predators. They are the top of the food chain, and their appetite puts every living being on the menu."

"It's like the Blackblood virus from the Holy Crusades then," Nikolai analogizes, speaking on some historical event I've never learned about.

"I can assure you, these creatures are far more sinister than any Blackblood you've read about in a history book. This creature would hunt Marduk down and make him beg for mercy, then eat his heart while his dying eyes watch. What makes them worse than Blackbloods is the possibility of contagion. Sure, there are a few million Undead the last census accounted for, but there are hundreds of millions of humans. If this disease reached the Areopagus, it would be the end of civilization as we know it. It would spread exponentially, effectively turning all we know and love into a second Deadlands."

"How the hell did you catch this thing and bring it here?" I ask. "I mean, if they're really that dangerous, wouldn't it be impossible to trap one when you finally returned from your voyage fifteen years later?"

"That's the thing... We didn't know we trapped one," Dyran replies with sadness in his voice. "When we reached the Deadlands, the natives set fire to our boats while we were out exploring the land. Our rations, our weapons, our way home, all of it went up in a plume of smoke. We had to learn how to live off the land, and when the sun set, we had to learn how to survive being hunted. Fifteen years is how long it took for us to build a new boat. The process was rife with setback after setback. The natives were hostile; they didn't want anything that discovered their land leaving to relay it to others. To them, we were sent as a sacrifice from the Creator for their demented gods. So when they discovered the construction of our boat was complete, they made sure the Wendigos knew.

"They attacked as we set off. After fifteen years, we had learned how to fight back against them long enough to evade death, but this was like nothing I'd ever seen before. The only leverage we had over them was the high ground. As they scaled the sides of our boat, we were able to knock them off into the icy waters below, but there were hundreds of them. One of them managed to get aboard. It decimated the few survivors we had left before I managed to kill it.

"In the fifteen years I survived the Deadlands, it was only thanks to a native woman who took me and my men in. Through their customs, she became my wife. She taught us how to survive, taught us how to stand our ground against the predators. But as we embarked on our journey, I learned she'd been bitten during the attack on our departure. I didn't have it in me to kill her. I didn't just love her, I owed her my life. So when the time came to make a decision, I trapped her in chains instead of killing her, then was forced to watch the disease consume her body into a monster I didn't recognize.

"That's who's in the mines, and that's who will slaughter this army of Undead. A shadow of my first and last love. The monster who still holds my heart."

"Love won't save us if Solis rises before we unleash your wife," Silenius interjects for the first time in a half hour. Until now, he's silently listened from the shadows while we created our scheme. I nearly forgot he was here, even though he is the upper echelon of royalty. "We need to get going, but I need to ask... What's the contingency if these Undead can't stop the monster we let loose?"

"Letting it find a way off this island isn't an option. If they can't kill it, we will have to," Dyran says, muffling his voice as he acknowledges what his heart doesn't want to accept.

"And if that's the case, will you be able to separate from your emotions for your wife for the greater good of mankind?" Silenius asks.

"I'll have to," Dyran admits in a whisper. "There's no other choice."

"Very good," Silenius confirms. "We Sylvians have a saying, a creed, if you will—'Vere mori skathen'—it means 'we conquer our demons.' Let's conquer some demons tonight."

25

FEAR IS GOOD

Nikolai carries me through the air, making me feel like I can fly for the first time in my life. This isn't like the time I battled with Ventur, when I plummeted to the ground toward certain death. In Nikolai's arms, I feel tranquil, euphoric even. Though war erupts beneath us, though hundreds of men march toward their deaths, I suddenly fear no evil in Nikolai's embrace. My anxiety washes away in the night breeze. It's from this aerial view that I realize how small I truly am, how small we all are.

As soon as we land outside the nearest mineshaft, we set to work making our primitive trap. It doesn't need to be perfect; it just needs to be enough to injure Count Viren and prevent him from flying away. The Wendigo can't fly like the Undead, so we need the Count to remain grounded. The margins of error for this trap are razor thin, hopefully thin enough to cut the strings that hold Viren's soul anchored on earth.

Nikolai and I land at the base of Dyran's armory, the building he showed us from the cliff's edge.

It's understandable how this quarry was the nation's largest producer of silver; the sheer size and scale of this crater seems big enough to swallow a distant star whole. It is like a poorly sculpted cereal bowl sitting in the ground. Its sides are uneven and jagged, climbing up to the surface in zigzagged steps taller than thrice my height. Caves litter the base like ventilation shafts, but these caves have been sealed shut by Dyran for some time now with boulders and heaps of crushed rock. Along the center of the crater is a manmade lake; the perfect place for rainwater to drain so none of the operation equipment is damaged.

But the operation equipment is broken nonetheless from being left unused for several years. Assembly lines filled with ore no longer run; the hand cranks used to rotate assembly belts are rusted into corroded disrepair. Heaps of chipped ore sit everywhere, making the crater's field look like a child who's constructed makeshift mountains in their playpen.

Spread out along the edge of the crater are buildings that used to have purpose for running day-to-day operations, but now they are a refuge for Dyran's forces. Steel towers loom over the mines, which I assume was used for miners to oversee production and micromanage their laborers.

The chaos of battle drowns out my thoughts. The crater is now a battlefield between Dyran's dwindling army and Viren's bloodsuckers. Dyran explained to Nikolai and I that most of his soldiers aren't battle hardened. They are citizens of Skaar he took in and put to work in exchange for shelter and food; only a small minority of them are survivors he brought back from the Deadlands, seeing his original Conquerers party was ravaged in the fifteen years they spent overseas.

Because of this, the Undead make short work of the inexperienced fighters. Screams erupt from everywhere, and the crater's looming walls reverberate them back onto the battlefield, making them add to the atmosphere of impending doom. Despite Nikolai's experience on his childhood blood-bag farm, most humans don't bend the nape willingly, and these fighters don't go to their deaths silently. Bodies fly everywhere, even human ones. The Undead pick them up and toss them around like playful projectiles.

Torches wave fire and smoke all around us, warming the night in an attempt to ward away the evil spirits. The Undead have no love for heat, but it is in no way a deterrent so long as there's fresh blood to be spilled.

Dyran's 'armory' is no more than an old, decrepit shed where I assume smiths used to make and repair pickaxes for mining. The furnaces where ore was once melted down to a more refined form are cold and dusty. Chains of varying lengths and sizes hang from the ceiling attached to pulleys and levers throughout the warehouse. Neglected pickaxes lay askew across tables and benches, and a few dozen are mounted on the walls like proud displays.

"This is perfect, we have everything we need," I say, staring at the chains and pulleys.

"I'm not a huge fan of this plan," Nikolai whispers, grabbing hold of a rusted chain in his hand. "I'm no mathematician, but there are negative odds this works."

"Listen, all you need to do is spring the trap. Let me handle the rest," I assure.

"Hey! What are you two doing in here?" a voice calls from the armory's entrance. Nikolai and I spin around at the same time, our voices catching in our throats. Standing in the door's frame is a bloodied man with shredded clothes. He leans on the door frame, almost like he's too weak to stand on his own.

"You're... you're Undead!" he screams, pointing at Nikolai. The man leans forward and picks up a pickaxe off the ground. He screams, hobbling toward Nikolai on one leg, "Come here you damn bloodsucker!"

Nikolai looks at me with bewilderment in his eyes. He doesn't know what to do. He knows I don't approve of Undead harming humans, but now it's Nikolai's life that's on the line.

"Stop!" I shout, jumping in between Nikolai and his aggressor.

"Out of my way, wench! I'll save you from this demon spawn!"

The bloodied man trips over the corner of a table, then falls to the ground. I bite the inside of my cheek as his head strikes an anvil, which opens his skull and spills what little blood remains in his body on the ground. The pickaxe bounces on the ground and lands at my feet. Nikolai passes me and kneels beside the dead man, running his finger through the fresh blood on the ground and bringing it to his lips.

"Stop!" I shout, running to remove him. "What do you think you're doing?"

Nikolai looks up at me as I ridicule him, startled. His lips are stained red from the poor bastard's blood. "What do you mean what am I doing? The dead have no use for blood... You expect me to turn down a free meal?"

"You're disrespecting a corpse..." I stutter, my worldview utterly in conflict with Nikolai's. To him, this is a kindness. Instead of having to feed on the living, he is making do with the scraps of the dead. But to me, there's something oddly perverse about drinking the blood of someone who's passed on from this life. He doesn't know this man, his life, his experiences, his hardships. He is a vulture, a parasite in the food chain who thrives because someone could no longer survive.

But as Nikolai slowly lowers his finger back to the ground for a second taste, I say nothing this time. In one way, he's right. The dead have no use for blood, and Nikolai will need his strength for what's to come.

I avert my eyes and begin assembling my weapon. When Nikolai is fed and his lips are licked, he deconstructs several pulley systems, coiling their chains in a tidy pile for later. My weapon is an evolution of everything I've become skilled at since being drafted, and some that I've learned from others.

I fashion a rope dart from thin, lightweight chains, but I draw inspiration from Celeste's whip for its ending. Instead of fastening a single dagger to a single chain, I knot a single chain into an intersection where it branches off with nine more chains, each one ending with a wooden dagger from my thigh holster. Nikolai affirmed what Garmin taught me—wounds an Undead receives from a wooden stake cannot be healed. Everything else is subject to rapid regeneration rates. Broken bones, torn muscles, lacerated flesh, all of it can heal with enough time. But there are two things an Undead fears worse than anything in this world—a wooden stake and daylight.

My decision to make my rope dart similar to Celeste's whip is twofold. First, Viren is undoubtedly faster than me. Striking him with a single dagger fixed on the end of my chain puts all my hope in ensuring he can't catch it. Having nine daggers coming for him at the same time though? That's a different story. And second, the goal is to subdue Viren, not kill him. By weaving these nine chains together, I don't really need to puncture Viren's flesh for the trap to be effective. I've effectively created a web of links that can wrap around any one of his limbs, and so long as Nikolai does his part, there's no way Viren will be able to take flight and evade capture.

As we leave the armory we know we need to act fast. Fighting ensues all around us. There are Undead all around who would gladly kill me, and there are humans who would gladly kill Nikolai. We stick to the shadow-concealed outskirts of the crater, shuffling along the wall toward the mineshaft we chose in advance from afar.

Some shafts are sealed off with insurmountable heaps of smashed rock, but others are covered with intact boulders. We choose the latter option as the place to spring our trap. Nikolai takes to the sky with his pulleys and mallet, quickly pounding the pulley rods into the rock above the cave mouth with his superhuman strength.

I, on the other hand, get to working on the spring that will trigger the trap. I grip an eye hook and start banging it into a nearby boulder that sits a few dozen feet in front of the sealed cave opening, working at half the speed as Nikolai with my frail strength.

You need to nail it lower, Wisteria growls, startling me. The mallet smashes into my thumb, causing me to scream inwardly. I yell at her in a whisper, channeling my pain and rage toward her, "Where the fuck have you been? I've needed you!"

You seem to be doing fine on your own, she purrs, calm as ever. Her yellow eyes drown out the purple stars that fly about in the distance. *I appear only when your mind manifests me, and your mind only manifests me when you doubt your abilities.*

"Don't make me sound like some scared child," I spit at her, annoyed by her statement. I rack my brain for truth in the assertion though, thinking of all the times she's been by my side. "I'm not scared right now," I defend, almost as if I'm trying to convince myself of that.

It's nothing to be ashamed of, child. Fear is good. It prepares you for what must be done—makes you stronger. Fear is your ally.

"Only the weak fear. I'm not weak anymore!" I shout, then look over my shoulder at Nikolai to ensure he doesn't overhear me talking to myself. He still floats over the mine's opening, busy constructing our trap.

Stop talking to me like you have something to prove. You've proved yourself a thousand times over since summoning me. What happens tonight won't change how proud of you I am.

"I... Wait, what? Did you just say... You're—"

I'm proud of you, Drakini. For how far you've come. For what you've overcome. For the decisions you've made. When your fellow human cried out for help, you rushed to their aid, despite me telling you not to. Now that, my child, is bravery—ignoring that voice in the back of your head that tells you to run and hide when the right thing to do is also the hardest path to take. It was in that moment I knew... You don't need me anymore, child, even in the moments you do feel fear.

"Wait, no... I still need you... I would be dead without you... I'd be in the infantry without you... I... I..."

And yet, it's my time to go, for if I appeared every time you felt the slightest fear in life, I would always be by your side. You created me from necessity—so you could cope with the suffering of life... My purpose is, and always has been, not to show you that there's nothing to fear, but to prove you are capable of overcoming anything that incites it. You're not weak. You've never been weak. Your only mistake was letting this world convince you otherwise.

"Please, don't go..." I stammer, the fear in my chest rising. The hairs on the back of my arms raise. Anxiety wells in my gut like a cyclone. "I need you... I... Please..."

"Drakini?" Nikolai calls from behind, startling me a second time. "Who are you talking to?" I spin around to face him, concern written on my face. As we lock eyes, Nikolai stumbles backwards, tripping over his feet and falling on his ass. "Damon's death!" He shouts, "Your eyes! What the... What's wrong with your eyes?"

I look away from him, back to where Wisteria stands, only to find that the hellcat has vanished from sight. I squeeze my eyes shut, feeling a torrent of emotions washing over me. Fear and bravery; fatigue and rejuvenation; weakness and strength. When I look at Nikolai once more, his face communicates a certain fear he feels toward me.

"What's wrong?" I ask, standing from the boulder to face him fully.

"What do you mean what's wrong?" He points eerily up at my face, trying to find words for what can't be described. "Your eyes, Drakini... They're amber!"

My eyes are amber? The statement makes sense faster than it probably should. Wisteria's eyes were amber, and now she has dissolved from reality and merged back into my shattered brain from whence she came. Before that, my eyes were a dull shade of shit brown. Could it be possible for my appearance to change now that she's reentered my body?

That wouldn't make any sense...

She was just a figment of my imagination, after all. But the fear on Nikolai's face is real, so the color of my eyes must really have changed.

We don't have time to waste on this, I realize. The night is only so long, and we still have much we need to do. I reply coldly, determination in my voice, "And yours are purple. Get over yourself, we have more pressing matters to address."

I extend my hand to help him up, which he accepts reluctantly. When he releases my palm, I take a wooden dagger from my rope dart and drag its sharpened tip across my palm, cutting it open wide enough to drown an anthill with my blood. I grit my teeth in pain; Nikolai swallows the excess salivation that gathers along his tastebuds.

"Get the boulder off the ground," I whisper, staring at him with my violently yellow eyes. The appetite he feels at the smell of my blood disappears as we lock eyes once more. He's scared of me, I realize. Wisteria's spirit now resides inside of me, and her eyes shine through for the outside world to see. I see now what she meant. She no longer needs to make herself known to me outside my body, because I now know she's been inside me this whole time.

"Right," Nikolai replies, jumping into action. "Right away!"

I turn away from him toward the fighting in the distance. I grab my rope dart with my lacerated palm, dragging its links through the blood that flows from my hand, then twirl the bloodied links through the air. Undead have a keen sense of smell for blood, and I now send the scent of mine into the air like a tornado. Viren will undoubtedly catch wind of it, and when he does, I'll be ready for him.

26

IF YOU WANT BLOOD, SUCK ON YOUR OWN

"What a wonderful scent you bleed into the air," a voice calls from the air above me, its narrator dropping to the earth. "I've always found the best way to celebrate a victory in battle is with a hard-earned meal."

I lay on the ground as Count Viren approaches me, holding onto my leg like I'm injured. The Count is unaccompanied by companions; his fighters snuff out the battle in the distance, sending the remainder of Dyran's forces to their deaths. I look up as Viren's silhouette blocks out the moon above. He twists his head in amusement as I look up at him, taking in his daunting figure. "How peculiar! A human with yellow eyes... Now that's something I can say I've truly never seen before. You mongoloids never cease to amaze me, even after all these years."

"Who... are you? What's happening?" I ask, making my voice unbearably feeble. I need to sell my vulnerability as I lay in the dust. Men are strong. Women are weak. It's the way the gods made us. Viren has no reason to question my weakness. This is the worldview he adopts. Humans are below him, and women are even lower than that.

"Seems like you've gotten yourself lost from the tournament, darling," Viren sneers at me. "I told my son to hunt down the humans in the contest, but it seems like you slipped through the cracks somehow. No matter, I'll fix that."

Viren just openly admitted to telling Ventur to kill all humans sent to this island as a part of the draft. That's why he was trying to draw us in with the screams of a fellow human. It wasn't just because he hates us; it's because his father put him up to it, I realize. *Being the son of a Count comes with pressure, and I fear it's done more harm to Ventur than anything,* Nikolai said.

"We... Silenius sent us..." I stammer, playing the idiot Viren sees me as. "Told... Told us to kill... Dyran..."

"Shhhh," Viren whispers through a malevolent smile that exposes his upper fangs. His mouth is stained red, indicating he's already had quite a few celebratory meals during battle. "There there, child. I'll put an end to your suffering, you poor thing..." He looks at me from head to toe, seeing the blood I've smeared along my clothes and flesh. It likely looks like I've been mauled by a Lycan, but I needed to sell this performance to make him think I'm injured. I need his guard lowered if I want a shot at trapping him, and I'm pleased to see his guard is now nonexistent now that my blood's hit his nostrils.

"What... What are you going to... do to me?" I cry aloud, somehow able to fabricate tears through some miracle.

"Just be still, child. I'm going to take the pain away..." For an Undead, Viren is wickedly handsome. I see now where Ventur gets his looks from. His face is stoic from a lifetime consuming solely blood; from his brows to his jawline, everything is chiseled. He has the features of a hawk on the hunt; his eyes devour me with their amethyst gaze. He wears a suit of skintight, midnight armor, though it cuts off at his collarbone so his beautiful face can be bathed in moonlight. His hair is as silver as the stars above and the ore deposited in the crater around us.

I shuffle my body away from him as he approaches, dragging myself through the dust like a worm trying to escape a bird of prey. Viren's senses are dialed in on me, drowning out his surroundings like a fool. He sees me as nothing more than a candidate of the draft that's been defeated by this hellish island. That's his mistake, I think to myself as I grab hold of the rope dart I've concealed in the dust of the earth. I let out a feral scream as I flip onto my feet faster than Viren can react, coiling my whip behind me and sending it arcing in his direction.

The smile on his smug face is replaced quickly by a look of surprise, then one of reaction. He kneels under the rattling chains as they whiplash where his head was, the wooden daggers stabbing nothing more than empty air. He pushes off from the ground and takes flight to close the distance between us, tackling me off my feet. His shoulder plants in my gut and throws me to the ground, weapon still in hand.

As I land with a discouraging thud, I'm forced to listen to his manic laughter erupt. He nearly doubles over with how hysterical he finds the transaction of events. I, on the other hand, don't find any humor in the situation.

"You humans! Man oh man, clever as foxes you are! Almost had me there, ya little bloodbag. Now come on, stop fooling around. This will all be much easier if you just submit to me," Viren says, his voice trailing off into a violent growl.

I pick myself up and brush myself off, readying my rope dart for a second go. I spit at the ground near his feet, smiling wide now as the rush of battle adrenaline seizes me. Viren has many things over me—strength, experience, speed—but there's one thing he doesn't have, and that's a demon inside him fiercer than mine.

I twirl the chain around my body fast, faster than even Viren can comprehend. With the extra weight of nine daggers on its end, it has enough momentum to make even me question its location at any given second. I send the chain out in his direction, baiting him to sidestep the attack, which he does arrogantly. "Is that the best you've got?" he shouts at me, still overwhelmed with laughter. I yank the chain back into my body and ride it's momentum, rotating my body to send it out a second time, then third, then fourth, each time allowing it to pick up more and more speed. I am like a scorpion, and my chain is a merciless tail striking my enemy until they feel my stinger.

I use my thighs, forearms, and armpits to move the chain from vertical strikes to horizontal, then back to vertical. I windmill it back and forth in different directions, grabbing a dagger from my thigh holster as Viren's eyes transfix on the chain's path of destruction. I release the chain, letting it dart out toward him again. This time, he ducks under it, and while his head is down I fling the loose dagger in my hand. The wooden stake hits its intended mark, burying into his clavicle, right above where his armor cuts off. Viren lets out a seething grunt as the sharpened wood buries itself below his neck.

"If you want blood, suck on your own," I scream at him. When Wisteria first appeared to me, she had to slow down time for me to achieve victory. I need no such help today; I will beat this bloodsucker in real time, I purr inwardly.

I flip over the chain as it flies back in my direction, using my body's momentum and trajectory to send it back for Viren's midsection. Agonizing over the pain of his wound, Viren doesn't dodge this strike, instead opting to bat it away with his forearm, which is exactly what I wanted. As his gauntlet knocks away the whip, the chains wrap themselves around his arm several times, tightening as I pull with all my might. This provokes Viren, sending him into a fit of rage as he moves to take flight.

As his feet lift from the ground, I dive to my side, clipping the hook at my end of the chain to the eye hook I buried into the immovable boulder.

"Dad!" a voice calls from the distance. When I look to the horizon, I see Ventur descending the crater's wall, his eyes glued on his cruel father. Viren fixes his eyes on his son for the briefest moment, which allows me to finish the trap. I retrieve a second chain, this one buried in the dirt beside the boulder, and clip it onto the eye hook, then kick the eye hook loose so it falls to the ground.

"Nikolai! Now!" I scream manically, staring back at the cave's open mouth. A set of purple eyes reveal themselves from the shadows of the open mine, the boulder that once blocked it now sitting upon a cliff above bound by a thick chain and multiple pulleys.

By the time Viren looks away from Ventur and his eyes follow where the chains lead, it's too late. Nikolai flies to the cliff the boulder sits on and swiftly kicks it. It already teeters on the crater's edge, so Nikolai's pressure is enough to send it tumbling over through the open air. The chain around it goes taut, then pulls the chain through the pulley system until it tightens Viren's leash and pulls him through the open air.

It's said Undead have remarkable strength, but with no ground beneath Viren's feet to dig into, he is unable to resist the pressure around his wrist. The chain tightens and yanks Viren's body toward the mine's open mouth as the boulder comes crashing down. Every foot the boulder moves, Viren is pulled three.

The Count lets out a shrill cry as he's whisked away into the darkness of the mineshaft, his scream no doubt calling out to any monster that lurks within. The boulder hits the ground where it previously sat, chains rattling as it seals the mineshaft off once more. Viren's scream is cut off as the boulder traps him where the moon can't shine. He will be safe in there from the coming daylight, but unfortunately for him, it's been nearly ten years since Dyran's wife has tasted flesh.

She will come for him, and when she does, my only regret will be not being able to hear his cries for help.

"What have you done!" Ventur screams, throttling his body through the air aimed directly at me. "I'll eat your heart out for this!" For some reason, the threat reminds me of Grite and forces me to laugh, which throws tinder on Ventur's flaming rage.

I throw myself to the ground and roll over my shoulder to avoid Ventur's initial assault. "Is that the best you've got?" I ask, mimicking his father as I grab hold of two daggers from my thigh holster. Ventur hits the ground, sending a plume of dust into the air. All I can see when he turns is his malevolent, amethyst eyes through the cloud of rocky residue that floats around him.

"Time to pay the piper, bloodbag whore," he hums from the smoke, his eyes seething. "I am next in line to be Count for Tribe Celestial. With my Undead soldiers, I will hunt you to the ends of the earth, deplorable human. I won't stop until I've squeezed every drop of blood from your veins like a tube of toothpaste. I'll squeeze the juices from your heart like a dishrag. I'll inseminate your corpse with my seed and mold your skull into the crown I wear as Count!"

"I did this kingdom a service by killing your father," I exclaim, swallowing my fear completely. "If you so much as touch me, I'll ensure your bloodline ends with you, bloodsucker."

He screams, charging forth from the rocky debris and into the fray of battle. Rage blinds him to his surroundings, so he never sees Nikolai coming from the cliffside where the boulder dropped. I don't bother flinching. I want my unafraid, human glare to be the last thing Ventur sees. I want him to know no matter what fear he tries to inflict, we humans won't run from cowardly men like him.

I lock eyes with him and stand defensively. I hope when he looks into my eyes, he sees the inconsolable hatred I hold for him in my yellow irises. I hope he knows that even if he hunts me to the ends of this earth, I will be waiting for him, silently waiting for our reunion, waiting to show him how weak he truly is.

In Nikolai's hands is an oversized rock the size of a watermelon, and it explodes into shards and dust as he thrusts it into Ventur's head. I smirk devilishly as Ventur's body loses all animation instantly. His face hits the ground so hard that I can hear his nose break. Nikolai cheers wildly, landing in front of me, "Take that, you fucking twat! I've been wanting to do that since he kicked me off a roof to see if I could fly as a kid." Nikolai smiles almost wider than me, letting out a sigh of celebratory wind.

Without prompting, we grip each other in a tight embrace. Both our bodies vibrate with a mix of adrenaline and excitement. As much as it would have brought me joy to put an end to Ventur's pride myself, Nikolai's actions have ushered in a new age of coexistence—proving it may actually be possible for humans and Undead to live in unity. Though he didn't choose humanity over his own species when Celeste whipped Myre to the brink of death, I see now how far he's come.

Nikolai and I are proof we can be more than the preconceived notions society has set. Women can be strong, just as much as men can be cowards. And Undead can be kind, just as much as humans can be cruel. Though we stand in a valley of death, our future on this earth is brighter than the moon above. And—

A loud boom erupts from the distance, causing Nikolai and I to release our grip on one another. For a moment we lock eyes, afraid to confirm what we've just heard. Together, we slowly look toward the base of the cliff where Nikolai dropped the boulder, and together, we see the tremendous rock that required a dozen pulleys to be lifted rolling away.

"Run!" Dyran screams from off in the distance. Nikolai jerks me back into his arms and jumps, taking flight as I watch the ground below us. Through the dust of war and the bleakness of night, I watch in horror as the boulder is thrown from its resting place, revealing the sinister frame of something not even the gates of hell could conceal. "Oh my gods," I whisper under my breath as a shriek of a feral predator paralyzes the night. A hundred purple eyes avert from their destruction toward the emerging figure, none of them quite knowing what the source of such a scream could be.

Dyran scales down the side of the crater as the Undead descend upon the monster, and the monster makes them pay for the sins they've committed on this treacherous night. My eyes can't believe what they're seeing as the beast known as the Wendigo does what Wendigos are diseased to do—hunt.

The feeling of victory quickly fades away as I see the power of what one creature is capable of and the death that follows in its wake. Nikolai and I land on the crater's edge where we first departed, rejoining Silenius's side once more. I don't dare look back down at the valley below, knowing I won't like what I see as the predator continues to send its triumphant scream into the night, shaking the trees around us. Instead, I watch Silenius's face react to the carnage that ensues. I silently reflect on the fact that I'm likely the first person in the Areopagus who's seen a Sylvian's face drain ghastly white.

"Oh Creator of malevolence, what have you done?" Silenius whispers to himself. The predator's screech continues to echo, and echo, and echo. The Undead below don't even have time to beg for mercy. And there Dyran stands, waiting to end it all.

27

HUNTRESS

Life no longer feels real, after being through what I have. It's almost an illusion. A human's brain isn't meant to withstand the supernatural world to this degree, yet I've made it through the draft nonetheless. I sit here, waiting for my name to be called so I can cross the stage and receive a medal with my assignment designation. King Silenius himself hands out the medals. He puts on a fake smile for the crowd, but I can see right through it.

What we witnessed on that island will haunt us for the rest of our lives. The natural order of this world will never be the same now that we've discovered a new apex predator in the food chain. The military branch known as the Hunters suddenly seems like humanity's last chance at survival, and my desire to be assigned to them has only flourished after the events of Skaar Island.

Around me are those humans who survived Skaar. A little less than 300 remain after the carnage, yet the Wendigo is not responsible for our losses. Celeste and her delinquent army of Undead went on that night to continue their quest for blood while Nikolai and I put an end to Viren. Dozens of soldiers with untapped potential joined Dante in the afterlife due to the Undead. Us humans who remain will never forgive for what they've done, and we will never forget.

The Undead will receive their assignments tonight. Silenius did this on purpose, as he knows I can no longer be in the same place as Ventur at the same time. Enmity between him and I will never end. He's called for a blood duel—says it's his entitlement to face his father's killer in a fight to the death. Now that Ventur is Tribe Celestial's newest Count, Silenius needs him in order to maintain control over the Undead. Now that Dyran is dead, I am the only human to witness the secrets this kingdom hides. Silenius needs us both, and will do whatever's necessary to keep us separated.

If it wasn't for Dyran, there's no telling how many of us would have died that night. In the nights since returning to Areopagus, I see his valiant stand when I close my eyes, and I see his crushed, bloodied body in my nightmares.

The Wendigo did what Dyran predicted it would. Several hundred Undead tried to kill it, their combined hubris too large to admit defeat at the hands of a single opponent. The whole scene didn't make sense. I've never seen a single being capable of slaughtering hundreds of victims, much less victimizing the Undead themselves. I remember the optimism I felt as the Undead surrounded the predator... Surely, in my mind, there was no way for the Wendigo to survive such a fatal attack. I've come to learn Dyran's fear of the creature was more than justified.

The Wendigo is more than just a predator; it is the god of the hunt. If Dyran's account of its origin can be believed, the Creator did all he could to create something that can finally put an end to the children of Solis and Luna's eclipse. To think that creature used to be a human—Dyran's wife of all humans—is beyond the realm of horror. In the ten years Dyran kept that beast trapped, the disease, the curse in its body superseded the bounds of reality.

Its face was nothing more than bone, as if it had used its talons to scrape its flesh clean in order to sustain its own hunger throughout the years of captivity. Antlers sprouted from its temple like the branches of a dying tree rattling against my window on a stormy night. Its arms were long enough to stretch to the ground, effectively making it a quadruped. Its torso was emaciated and covered with fur, like it had skinned a Lycan and donned its pelt like some mangy cloak. Sharpened bones tore from its flesh like calcified stalagmites. Its entire body was more exoskeleton than flesh, like a walking, living, breathing skeleton of some demented elk. The demon's talons were elongated, making its grip wide enough to wrap fully around the skull of an Undead. Watching the beast move was like seeing a wintery forest of trees and moss and bone come to life.

Dyran laid down his life to dispense the killing blow against the woman he once loved, and no one but me and Nikolai and Silenius will ever know. Silenius covered up the events of that night exactly how he told us he would. The candidates of the draft were sent to Skaar Island to put an end to Dyran's rebellion, so the kingdom can resume the production of silver once more. There was no army of Undead sent, and the draftees weren't a distraction for Silenius to find Dyran. There was no assassination attempt on Count Viren's life. His body was never recovered from the mineshaft, and propaganda has already been spread to the Undead that his death resulted from a bloodbag slaying him in his sleep. Ventur may know the truth of his father's demise, but Silenius has made sure to silence him. After all, it would be unfortunate for the entire Celestial populace to learn their leader was actually killed by a sixteen-year-old human girl during active battle. To preserve his father's memory, Ventur is the last person we need to worry about leaking the truth.

Ventur is no stranger to keeping secrets. To this day, no one knows I beat him in our duel, and no one likely ever will. Silenius has already befriended the pompous soldier as a way of keeping him on a tight leash. Silenius plans on having him drafted into the Black Knights—the protectors of the crown. Then, Silenius will be able to keep a close eye on the untrustworthy bloodsucker, and now that Viren is dead and gone, Silenius can rule this kingdom free of outside control.

I've become invaluable as Silenius's confidant.

In the passing days since our return, he's called on Nikolai and I numerous times to weigh in on the affairs of this kingdom, even though we are nothing more than teenagers. Sometimes I forget Silenius is our age, and I can't imagine how lonely life as a king is. In many ways, I no longer feel like a common citizen from Fyrefell anymore. So much has changed in such little time. Memories of fetching water and tending to our homestead feel like a past life. Trauma has shaped and molded me, and instead of letting it break me, I've emerged stronger.

"Myre of Fyrefell—Ranger Corps," Silenius announces, breaking me from my daydream. I haven't had the chance to speak to him since Skaar Island. I visited him two days ago in the infirmary but he was incapacitated, his back stitched up with enough thread to knit a blanket. He limps from his seat and up to the stage to receive his medal. Silenius puts it on him delicately, knowing his back is too raw to bow for his king. It's a proud moment for us both. I can hardly recognize the boy who was once my best friend.

In the months we've been separated, he's sprouted like a weed, and his demeanor has changed dramatically. He is not the frail boy I used to defend from village bullies. The draft has changed him—hardened him into a man through adversity. We lock eyes as he crosses the stage. My heart drops as I see the vacancy in his stare. He is no longer the optimistic child that followed me around. Instead, I swap gaze with a hollow man who's been sent to hell and back.

The fact that Myre made it to the top 500 draftees is remarkable, especially because I know what it took for me to make it there myself. There were many qualified warriors in my military sector who didn't make the cut as the tournament pressed on, and I'd assume the military sector where Myre was sent had the same pool of talent. Still though, being chosen to be a Ranger is no small feat. Even if my eyes weren't set on the Hunters, I'm not sure I could make the Rangers. I've seen them drill in the practice yards before. Their athleticism is something I couldn't dream of possessing, which makes it hard to believe Myre has what it takes. The kid couldn't even catch a stickball a few months ago, let alone was he stealthy enough to go scouting for this kingdom.

But that's a part of growing up. All the good times I spent by his side, all the fond memories, all the laughter shared—none of it matters anymore now that we are strangers. Still though, I thank the gods he survived Skaar Island, and though it's been years since I've prayed to the gods, I will pray for Myre's wellbeing in the Ranger Corps.

Draftees continue being called across the stage. Most of their faces share little excitement after the horrors they've seen. The vast majority is drafted to the Mounted, though several receive the honor of becoming Black Knights—this kingdom's elite fighting force. Fewer are picked up by the Rangers and Marksman Corps, but those who are simply look like they belong there. The physique required to be a Ranger or Marksman is noticeably different from the behemoth builds of Mounted and Black Knights.

By the time my name is called to cross the stage, not a single person has been chosen to join the infamous Hunters, but that all changes with me.

"Drakini of Fyrefell—Huntress," Silenius calls out. Silence falls over the scattered whispers throughout the amphitheater. All eyes shift toward me. For some reason it feels like I'm a death row inmate walking toward the guillotine. But Silenius's silver eyes comfort me as I climb the stage and bow my head for him to bestow me with the medal. He whispers in my ear as I'm near him, low enough so no one can hear: "Hunters meeting in my chambers—sunset."

I nod curtly and exit the stage. Before Skaar Island, I wanted nothing more than to be a Huntress. But now that I've seen the kind of monsters that plague this world, it's hard to fake my smile as I retake my seat. I listen closely as the draft continues. By the time it ends, I am the only candidate to be designated to the Hunters.

28

WHAT MAKES ME HUMAN

"**I**'ve called you all here because we face a state of emergency," Silenius announces as he strides into his chambers. All around me are grim warriors who stand like silent shadows throughout the regal room. No two wear the same garb. Some wear sleeveless tunics, others have scattered armor. A man standing in the corner wears a somber mask resembling a demonic spirit, tusks extending from the jawline in an upper facing arc. Most of their pants are baggy to the knees and wrapped tight with kyjahans over their shins. Hooded cowls cover their lurking, mistrusting eyes. Since I've arrived, none have acknowledged my presence, and none have spoken to each other.

"I've debriefed all of you what actually happened on Skaar several nights ago," Silenius continues, his silver eyes floating from Hunter to Hunter. "There exists a new enemy, one far more dangerous than any of us in this room have hunted. Known as the Wendigo, the beast is believed to be the natural predator of Lycans and Undead alike. Plagued by a curse of the Creator, this creature has the ability to not only destroy all humanity's built, but to make humanity go extinct, which is why I've called you all here. Effective immediately, I am suspending all ongoing Hunter missions and making this our utmost priority. This group is civilization's last hope—I'm sending you on a mission to the Deadlands to find and eradicate the scourge known as the Wendigos. Your newest member Drakini, this groups' first ever Huntress, has seen firsthand what this demon is capable of..."

I pause in my tracks, drowning out Silenius's voice. Did I just hear him correctly? This groups' first ever Huntress? I look at the warriors around me, searching the crowd for some sign of another female. He's right, I realize. There are no women here—not that I can find at first glance at least.

Silenius continues, "The predator took out nearly a hundred Undead before being defeated. As of now, we know none of its weaknesses, nor do we know how to overcome it. This mission is one you may never return from. It will take everything you have. The Deadland natives are considered, at this time, hostile to our aims. As far as we know, they worship these monsters as their gods, and they will sacrifice you accordingly if you're caught. This is more than recognizance—you'll have to learn how to survive in this wasteland, you'll have to research your enemy, and you'll have to execute them accordingly. A party known as the Conquerers was sent by my father two and a half decades ago to navigate this land, and it was their bravery that led us to this discovery. As of today, not a single one of them is alive, and most perished before fleeing the Deadlands.

"I expect the results to be different from this group," Silenius admits, looking us over once more. "You all have spent your lives dedicated to hunting the monsters that endanger civilization. It's become your purpose in life. The outcome of this mission will rest solely on who the better hunter is—you or the Wendigo—and I have no doubt you will make the Creator answer for his sins against humanity."

I clench my fists and grind my teeth. My father told me in a past life this was coming, and it is finally here. *Men will put you in the dust and trample over you. And that is just the men. The Undead will do worse. They will feed on your blood until you are too weak to stand. They will leave you for the Lycans to pick your body apart like jackals. If you leave, you will die. If you leave, there will be no burial for your bones.*

The things he said weren't false, but he wasn't right either. There are monsters in this world, that's for sure. But they aren't invincible, and they don't have to be feared.

It is the law of nature that monsters only prey on those they can victimize, which means there's an alternative. I know this because I've started the process of making myself a monster. I may not have fangs or claws or a ghastly appearance, but I am still the one with the advantage. The reasons I hunt is not the same as these cursed beasts, who hunt for bloodlust and hunger and selfishness. The reason I hunt is simple... Somewhere, out there, the moon shines on someone too weak to defend themself. They are the reason I hunt. Because that's what makes me human, at the end of the day. It isn't the fact that I have no demon residing inside me, but that I make my demon fight for the betterment of mankind. That is what Lycans and Undead and Wendigos will never be capable of, and that is why I will one day be the greatest Huntress this world has ever seen.

ABOUT THE AUTHOR

As a child, Devin Thorpe once saw an action figure he wanted in Wal-mart. He stared at it in contemplation for quite some time, until his father interrupted him. "Well, are you going to get it?"

Devin looked at his father with reluctance, then answered, "I'm too old to play with toys now. I'll get made fun of at school if people knew."

His father looked at him sympathetically, then grabbed the toy off the shelf for him and put it in the shopping cart. As he walked away from Devin, he called over his shoulder, "I wish when I was your age my own father had taught me you can never be too old to play with toys."

Devin Thorpe attributes his imagination to his parents raising him in an environment where he could daydream without interruption, whether that was playing in the backyard with imaginary friends or buying action figures when he was entirely too old.

www.ingramcontent.com/pod-product-compliance
Lightning Source LLC
Chambersburg PA
CBHW032129170626
46808CB00006B/2156